Treasure
of Love

SCOTTY CADE

Dreamspinner Press

Published by
Dreamspinner Press
4760 Preston Road
Suite 244-149
Frisco, TX 75034
http://www.dreamspinnerpress.com/

Treasure of Love

Cover Art by Catt Ford

ISBN: 978-1-61581-945-4

Printed in the United States of America
First Edition
May 2011

eBook edition available
eBook ISBN: 978-1-61581-946-1

First and foremost, always to Kell, I love you.

And to my built-in Martha's Vineyard entourage, the BNO boys, Paul, Jonathan, Scott, Shawn, Justin, and Dudley, you guys have brought so much to our lives and your support and friendship means the world to us. Thank you!

Chapter *1*

SAFELY docked in Skagway, Alaska, and awaiting his next charter, Dive Master and Captain Jackson P. Cameron was spending a leisurely afternoon lounging on the deck of the *Lindsey C*, his seventy-five-foot dive boat. Soaking up the warmth of the Alaskan summer sunshine and enjoying the gentle sound of the waves lapping against the hull, he was debating on making a big change in his life. He'd been diving and doing charters for the last ten years and was hitting the burnout period. It wasn't a bad life, and he did get to do what he loved—diving and captaining his own boat—but his heart told him it was time for a change. Unfortunately, his wallet told him otherwise.

Everyone needs a change every now and then, damn it. This is my time, he thought. *Money or no money, when my next charter's done, I'm taking a few weeks off and heading to a warm, sunny climate to decide what I want to do with the rest of my life.*

His tranquility was suddenly interrupted by the voice of Johnny Horton singing the old country classic, "North to Alaska." *Why in the hell did I choose that stupid song as the ringer on my cell phone? God, I hope this isn't another charter.* He dug his phone out of the pocket of his khaki shorts, lifted it to his ear, and said, "Jack Cameron."

"Is this the Jack Cameron who owns the charter boat *Lindsey C?*" the caller asked.

"One and the same," Jack said. "And this is…?"

The caller said, "I'm Daxston Powers. I'm sure you've probably heard of me."

Jack did a quick scan of his mind's database. "Nope, can't say that I have," Jack responded. "But what can I do for you… Daxston, is it?"

"Yes, but you can call me Dax," the caller responded in an annoyed tone. "I would like to meet with you to discuss securing your boat for a long-term charter," he said.

"Really? How long is long-term?" Jack asked.

"I'm not completely sure. It depends on how long it takes you to find what I'm looking for. It could be a couple of weeks on the low end and up to three months on the high end."

Dollar signs flashed in front of Jack's eyes, and then the realization hit him. *There goes my time off.*

Not wanting to seem too anxious, he said, "I've got a pretty tight schedule, but sure, we can meet. When and where?"

"Where are you now?" Dax asked.

"I'm docked near the ferry landing in Skagway," he replied. "My next charter pulls away from the dock at two o'clock tomorrow afternoon."

"I'll be at your boat at ten a.m. sharp tomorrow morning," Dax said, and hung up the phone without waiting for a response.

"I'll be he—" Jack said as he heard a click in his ear before he could finish his sentence.

"Arrogant bastard," he said to himself as he looked at his cell phone.

He hit the "end" button and slipped the phone back into his pocket. He stretched out again for a second time and tried to place the name Daxston or Dax Powers, but nothing came to mind except *arrogant bastard.*

"North to Alaska, They're goin' North, the rush is on."

Damn, I really have to change that. He immediately felt a flash of guilt: *maybe the guy didn't hang up on me after all.* Without looking at the caller ID, he put the phone to his ear and started to speak.

"I guess we were disconnected."

He heard a short pause on the other end of the line. "Nope, try again," the caller said.

Jack immediately recognized the voice and smiled.

His former brother-in-law and best friend, Mac Cleary, was a floatplane pilot who now lived in Hiline Lake, Alaska, with his partner, retired oncologist, Dr. Bradford Mitchell. Mac had been happily married to Jack's sister, Lindsey, until she had died of cancer eight years ago. After being alone for over five years, Mac had unexpectedly reconnected and fallen in love with Brad, a former passenger. Brad had recently lost his partner, Jeff, to colon cancer, and the two men had formed an unbreakable bond, which over time had turned into love. Jack had had a hard time dealing with Mac's sudden change in lifestyle, but eventually he'd come to accept it, and if he was honest with himself, was a little envious of their loving relationship.

"Hey, Mac, what's up, man?"

"Not much, Jackie, just checking in. I haven't talked to you in over a week. Are you on a charter?"

"Not yet, but picking up a three-day run starting tomorrow afternoon."

"Good deal," Mac said. "Fishing or diving?"

"Diving," Jack responded. "Don't do much fishing anymore, it really takes a toll on the boat, and it's too damn messy. Hey, how's Bradford?" Jack asked.

"He's good," Mac said. "We just landed in Anchorage for an overnight trip to pick up supplies. We haven't left the lake since we got back from Europe, and we're starting to get down to the bare necessities."

"It must be nice to retire so young and have the means to go on one adventure after another, and then escape back into the solitude of the Alaskan mountains for weeks at a time to rest up," Jack said, with quite a bit of envy in his voice.

"It is nice, no doubt about that," Mac said. "But Brad's the one with all the money. Who would have thought that at this stage of my life I would be married to a rich doctor?"

"I need to find a rich doctor to take care of me," Jack added.

"Very funny," Mac said. "Just like you, Jack, to make me sound like a gold digger."

"I'm teasing," Jack said.

"I know," Mac admitted. "But we've been on the go for most of the last two years, and although I know he loves it when we get home, I can tell he's already starting to get cabin fever."

"You guys never let any moss grow under your feet, and I love that about you," Jack said. Jack heard Mac start to speak again, but his words faded into the background as he zoned out and stared out over the horizon. *It sure would be nice to have someone special to share my life with.*

"Jack? Did I lose you?" Mac asked.

"No, no, I'm here," Jack said. "Sorry, I zoned out for a minute, what did you say?"

"I was saying that I guess we're both enjoying life again," Mac confided. "Those five years after Lindsey died, I was barely going through the motions of living. And Brad, he was fighting so hard to cure Jeff's cancer, he thought of little else. And when Jeff had had enough of the unsuccessful treatments and decided he was ready to give up, Brad supported his decision and never left his side. I think a piece of us died with each of our partners, and we're just now starting to live again."

"I think you guys have been really good for each other," Jack shared. "It's no secret that it took me quite a while to get used to the idea of you two, you know, being together, but now I can't imagine you *not* being together."

Mac chuckled. "Oh, you don't have to remind me of how much of a pain in the ass you were," he said.

"Come on, Mac, that's water under the bridge," Jack said. "You seem happy now, and that makes me happy," Jack added, meaning every word.

"Thanks, Jackie," Mac responded.

"Not to change the subject, Mac, but have you ever heard of someone named Daxston Powers?"

"Daxston Powers," Mac mumbled to himself, certain he recognized the name. "Oh yeah, I think he goes by Dax," he said. "He's one of those modern-day treasure hunters."

"Really—a treasure hunter, huh?" Jack asked.

"Yeah. Brad and I just saw a documentary a couple of weeks ago on the Discovery Channel about his last expedition."

"The Discovery Channel. He must be pretty famous," Jack said.

"More *in*famous, I think," Mac responded.

"What do you mean?" Jack asked.

"Well, in a Geraldo-Rivera-finding-nothing-in-Al-Capone's-vault sort of a way," Mac responded.

"You lost me," Jack said.

"Let me see if I can get this right," Mac continued. "Last fall, Powers was off the coast of Cape Horn in search of a clipper said to be carrying a bounty of diamonds, rubies, and emeralds. I think it was called the *Sarah Maria*. And according to the documentary, the information surrounding the *Sarah Maria*'s demise had been so vague that she'd eluded treasure hunters for the last one hundred and fifty years."

Jack interrupted, "So I'm sure finding that wreck would help to validate his work and boost his career," he said.

"Pretty much," Mac continued. "He knew that if he found the wreck, he would garner some much-needed recognition and credibility to help him find investors for future expeditions."

"And that's why he invited the Discovery Channel to film the entire expedition," Jack added. "So, did he find the wreck?"

"Much like Geraldo found the vaults, he found a wreck, but unfortunately for him, it wasn't the *Sarah Maria*."

"Serves him right," Jack said.

"What?" Mac asked.

"Oh, nothing, go on," Jack responded.

"Okay, it's official, you're very weird," Mac teased. "But that's not the best of the story."

"There's more?" Jack asked.

"Oh yeah, on the last day of the failed expedition, they were caught off guard by an unexpected fall storm, and Dax's research vessel, *Hunter's Instinct*, went down in very high winds and pounding seas."

"No shit," Jack whispered through a smile.

"Yep, and the really impressive thing is that he stayed on board until everyone was safely rescued, barely escaping with his own life."

"The captain always goes down with his ship," Jack said. "Not a new concept."

"I still think it's pretty impressive," Mac added. "But once he was finally aboard the rescue boat, he swore, on camera, that he would get a new boat and he would continue his research until he found the wreck of the *Sarah Maria*."

"Did he now?" Jack asked as his mind started to wander again. *Did Powers want him to help them find the* Sarah Maria?

Mac spoke again, "I know this is a stupid question after all that, but what's this all about?"

"He just called me and wants to talk to me tomorrow morning about chartering the *Lindsey C* for as long as three months. And that's who I thought was calling me back when you called."

"No shit?" Mac said. "Certainly he doesn't want you to take the *Lindsey C* to Cape Horn?"

"Who knows what the arrogant bastard wants?" Jack admitted.

"Wow, I can see that he really made an impression on you," Mac said. "What did he do that has you in such a tizzy?"

Jack explained how their earlier conversation had started and abruptly ended.

Mac laughed and said, "They hinted in the documentary that he can be a little arrogant and somewhat difficult to work with."

"We'll just see how difficult he'll be when he hears my price. The *Lindsey C* is *my* boat and *I'm* the captain, not Daxston Powers. And what in the hell kind of a name is Daxston anyway?" Jack asked.

Mac laughed. "Oh man, he's in for it now. Give him hell, Jackie," he urged.

"Yeah, yeah, yeah," Jack said.

"Okay, Jack. Gotta run, Brad's waiting for me in the truck, but please give me a call after your meeting tomorrow morning. I'm dying to know what he has in mind."

"Will do, Mac, and give my best to Brad."

"I'll do it. Bye, Jack."

MAC hooked his phone back to his belt as he wondered if he should have mentioned to Jack that Dax was openly gay. *Nah, he'll figure it out sooner or later, and this could prove to be interesting.*

He thought back to the many conversations he and Lindsey had had before she died, about how they thought Jack might be gay. He'd been married for a few months some fifteen years ago and would never talk about what went wrong. Since then, he'd not had anything close to a serious relationship, nothing more than a date here or there, and when he'd found out about Mac and Brad, he'd thrown a fit and threatened to never talk to Mac again. Eventually he'd come around, but not without some major coaxing. At the time, Mac was new to the lifestyle as well, and didn't know the signs like he did now, but Brad's gaydar was on high alert from the start, and Jack's homophobia had only added to Mac and Brad's speculations about his sexuality.

Yep, this could prove to be very interesting.

Chapter 2

THE next morning, Jack was up and moving around by eight o'clock. He'd had a pretty restless night's sleep, so he'd slept in an hour or so longer than he usually did when he was in port. He poured himself his first cup of coffee and then walked out onto the deck and sat in his favorite spot on the bowsprit. He looked back over the *Lindsey C*, as he did every morning, and admired her sleek lines. Her dark-blue hull and highly polished teak trim against her bright white deck complemented the long, slim, tinted windows and high-tech bridge. His mind drifted back to his mysterious phone call yesterday and his conversation with Mac. *Dax Powers must be on a pretty hot trail if he can't wait until his new boat is ready. That could mean some serious money for me, and having a little nest egg put away could make my time off a little less stressful.*

He sipped his coffee while he anticipated what the day would bring. When his third cup was empty, he showered and made another pot for his guest. By nine fifty-five he was standing on the fly bridge, sipping his fourth cup, when a taxi pulled up to the dock. A tall man of over six feet, possibly in his late twenties, with dark brown hair cut short on the sides but a bit longer on top, unfolded out of the back of the small taxi. Jack watched who he assumed was Dax Powers stand, stretch, and lean his head into the driver's-side window. As he appeared to give the driver further instructions, the other door opened, and a tall, thin female, about the same age and with the same features, got out of the taxi as well.

Jack observed the two as they spotted the boat and made eye contact with him. Jack instinctively waved and smiled, and the woman acknowledged him and quickly waved back. Dax simply started walking toward the boat, glaring at him, never breaking eye contact. Jack noticed that, as they walked toward the boat, the woman appeared nervous and kept looking around like she thought they were being followed. The longer Jack watched, and the closer they got to the boat, the more obvious their resemblance became. *I'll be damned, they're twins.*

Jack reached the gangplank as his guests approached the boat, and stopped. He gave them the once-over, and they were indeed a beautiful pair. Jack wasn't in the habit of ogling men, but damn if Dax wasn't a strikingly handsome guy. He had full, pouty lips and the sexiest hazel eyes he'd ever seen—sultry and lazy, in a way that reminded him of a young Elvis Presley. Jack was mesmerized by Dax's eyes. The color was a mixture of brown, green, and amber, and they were sheltered by thick, long, dark lashes. Jack couldn't remember ever seeing eyes that color or eyelashes that long, especially on a guy, and he stared into them way too long for his own comfort. He broke away and turned to the woman accompanying Dax. She was just as strikingly beautiful, and although her eyes appeared to be more on the green side than brown or amber, there was no mistaking the fact that they were brother and sister. In addition, they both appeared to be very fit and looked so damn healthy, he made a mental note that he needed to increase his workouts.

He was startled when the woman said, "Permission to come aboard, Captain?"

"Permission granted," Jack responded with a smile.

"Captain Cameron?" she asked.

"In the flesh," Jack responded. "But please, call me Jack."

She stuck her hand out and said, "Okay, Jack, I'm Donatella Powers, and this is my brother Dax."

Jack shook and released her hand. "Nice to meet you, Donatella."

"Everyone calls me Dona."

Jack nodded, looked at Dax, and stuck his hand in his direction.

"Pleased to meet you, Dax," Jack said.

Dax looked at the outstretched hand, but didn't move. Dona sent a quick jab to his ribs with her elbow that seemed to startle him, and he hesitantly took Jack's hand in a very firm handshake. The kind of handshake Jack liked to call the "my dick is bigger than your dick" handshake.

"Welcome aboard the *Lindsey C*," Jack said.

"Thanks," Dona replied. "Is there somewhere private we can talk?"

"Let's head down to the salon, and we can talk there," Jack suggested.

Both Dona and Dax continued nervously looking around the dock as they made their way below deck.

He led them through the companionway and into a well-appointed, mahogany-lined salon with a black leather couch and two upholstered side chairs. There were built-in bookcases above the windows, port and starboard, and a flat-panel television on the wall above the navigation desk. Midship was a banquette across from the galley, and in between was a set of stairs leading to four forward sleeping cabins. Aft was another set of steps that went down to the master cabin.

They settled on the couch, and Jack asked, "Can I get you anything?"

"No thank you, I'm fine," Dona said. "You, Dax?" she continued. Dax shook his head no, so Jack sat down across from them.

"So what's this all about?" Jack asked.

"We are about to give you some very private information," Dona said as she reached into her backpack and pulled out a folder containing a stack of papers. She sorted through the papers until she found what she was looking for. She handed Jack a stapled document and said, "You'll need to sign this before we can really get into details."

Jack quickly scanned the two-page document titled "Nondisclosure Agreement." It was a simple, straightforward document stating that he could not disclose any information shared between them during this meeting or he would be held legally responsible. Dona held a pen in his direction, which he took and used to sign the agreement. He handed the document back to Dona, and she placed it back into the folder. Only then did Dax speak.

"Jack, I'm not sure if you are aware of this, but Dona and I recently lost our vessel while searching for the wreck of the *Sarah Maria* off the coast of Cape Horn."

Jack nodded. "Yeah, I heard about that. That was really a tough break."

The look on Dax's face tightened considerably, but he kept his composure as he continued.

"While doing further research on the *Sarah Maria*, we stumbled upon some documents that allude to the final resting place of a wreck here in Alaska called the *Anna Wyoming*."

"Why does that ring a bell?" Jack asked.

"She went down in the Lynn Canal, heading for Skagway, during the 1898 Klondike Gold Rush," Dax said.

"Oh yeah, I've heard of that wreck," Jack said. "Around here, that ship is old folklore. No one's been able to locate her in over a hundred years."

"Until now," Dax said.

Jack tilted his head and studied Dax's expression before Dax continued.

"Legend has it the boilers exploded, and she went down fast, carrying a shitload of gold," Dax explained. "But no one's been able to find her to prove that theory. And trust me, many have tried. We now have reason to believe that we have the approximate location of the wreck and have uncovered paperwork that proves that the gold was on that ship."

"How much gold?" Jack asked.

Dona and Dax looked at each other, and Dona said, "We're not one hundred percent certain, but it could be as much as ten million dollars in today's market."

Jack whistled. "That's a lot of money. So how do I fit into the picture?" he asked.

"We need your boat," Dax replied.

"Okay," Jack said. "What's in it for me?"

"Half a million when we recover the gold," Dax offered.

"Interesting," Jack said. "And if we don't recover the gold and this expedition turns out to be a bust like your last one?" he asked while staring at Dax.

Jack could see the anger building as the blood rushed to Dax's face. Dona touched Dax's arm—Jack assumed to keep him calm and remind him to keep his cool.

"No gold, no payout," Dax said.

Jack stood. "I'm sorry you wasted your time coming all the way out here," Jack said. "But your terms won't work for me."

"Okay, Jack. But just so we'll know… what terms *will* work for you?" Dona asked.

"A quarter of the take," Jack responded.

"Damn it!" Dax yelled as he slammed his fist on the table, stood, and looked at Dona. "I told you this was a bad idea."

Dona pulled Dax back down to his seat and looked at Jack. "Mr. Cameron."

"Please call me Jack," he said.

"Okay, Jack," Dona said. "Thank you for your time. You're the first captain we've talked to, so we'll just keep looking."

Jack stood. "Suit yourself," he said. "But I'm sure you've done your homework and already know that there's only one other charter boat within a two-hundred-mile radius, and he just got to Skagway last year. I've been navigating the Lynn Canal for the last ten years and know her waters well. So the way I see it, your options are very limited."

Dona looked at Dax, who seemed to have steam blowing out of his ears, then back to Jack. "Can you give us a minute alone?"

"Sure thing," Jack said as he walked out of the salon.

He climbed the stairs to the deck and released his breath. He couldn't believe he'd just negotiated his way into—he quickly did the math—two and a half million dollars.

Before he could revel in his victory, Dona and Dax were standing in front of him.

"Okay, Jack, we have a deal," she said.

Jack stuck out his hand to shake on it.

"Not so fast," Dax said. "We have a deal, under one condition."

Stunned, Jack pulled his hand back and said, "There's always a condition, isn't there?"

"You incur all the up-front expenses, such as fuel, provisions, and crew," he said. "And in the event we don't find the wreck at the end of our contract, we'll pay you for half of the incurred expenses and call it even."

"Half," Jack said.

"Yes, Jack, half. If you want a portion of the purse, you have to share some of the risk. It's only fair."

"I'll need some time to think about this," Jack said.

Dona looked at Dax. "We'll give you until six o'clock this evening. If we don't hear from you by six, we'll either look for another captain or bring in a boat from elsewhere."

"Okay," Jack said. "If I decide to take the expedition, I'll call you by six o'clock."

Dona handed Jack a business card with her cell phone number on it, and she and Dax left the boat in much the same way they had arrived—keeping a watchful eye and looking around nervously as they got back into the cab and drove off. Jack immediately removed his cell phone from his pocket and started dialing.

MAC and Brad were loading their floatplane with supplies after their morning of shopping in Anchorage when Mac's cell phone rang. Mac looked at the caller ID and smiled.

"Jack, I've been on the edge of my seat all morning. What happened?"

"Is Brad with you?" Jack asked.

"Yeah, he's right here, why?"

"Can you put your cell phone on speaker?"

"Yeah, hang on."

Mac hit the speaker button and held the phone out so he and Brad could hear what Jack had to say.

"You won't believe this shit, guys."

"Tell us," Mac said.

Jack filled Mac and Brad in on the entire conversation, except for the details of the wreck—mainly, the name and potential location—at least trying to stick to the nondisclosure agreement.

When he was through telling the story, there was silence on the other end.

"Guys, are you still there?" Jack said.

"We're here," Brad said. "We just can't believe it."

"I know what you mean," Jack replied. "Here comes the good part."

Brad and Mac listened intently as Jack continued.

"Do you guys want to crew the boat with me?" Jack asked.

Before Mac could answer, Brad said, "Hell, yeah."

Mac laughed and said, "Well, I guess you have your answer."

Jack chuckled. "Now listen, guys, there will be work involved. You'll have meals to prepare, laundry to wash, decks and equipment to clean, and all the other stuff that goes along with a charter."

"No problem," Brad said. "When do we leave?"

"Don't know yet. They don't even know I've accepted the job."

"When will you let them know?" Brad asked.

"I have until six o'clock tonight to let them know, but I'm pretty damn sure they'll want to leave as soon as possible."

Mac jumped in. "Wait a minute, what do we get out of this?"

"You mean besides the adventure of a lifetime?" Jack said.

"Well yeah. I mean, it sounds like fun, but it will be work."

"Okay, here's the deal that Dax and Dona and I agreed to," Jack explained. "I get a quarter of the take, which could be as much as two and a half million dollars, but I have to cover all the up-front expenses. And if we come up empty-handed, they will only cover half of what I've already spent."

"That sucks," Brad admitted.

"But to lower my risk and make this a little easier on my wallet, what if I give you a quarter of my take, which could be upwards of seven-hundred-and-fifty-thousand dollars, and in return, if we do come up short, you pay for half of my half of the expenses? That way, each of us is only on the hook for a quarter of the expenses."

"Deal," Brad shouted.

Mac chuckled. "Can we at least talk about this, Brad?" he asked.

Brad gave Mac the pleading look he'd seen so many times in the last few years.

"I guess we're in," Mac said. "Let us know when they want to leave."

Jack heard Brad yell at the top of his lungs, but couldn't see the kiss that followed. "Will do," he chuckled. "Now I've got to call the Powers's, and tell them we'll take the gig."

"Hey, Jack, before you hang up," Mac yelled. "Was Powers as much of an asshole as you thought?"

"He far exceeded my expectations," Jack responded.

Jack heard Mac laughing in the background and Brad still yelling as he ended the phone call. *I guess they really were ready for another adventure.*

JACK spent the rest of the day readying his boat for the three-day charter he had to get through before they would embark on their new adventure. His thoughts drifted between the details of the expedition and fantasizing about the money and what he would do with it. He took a gamble and waited until five after six to call Dona. He didn't want to seem too anxious, but if he was honest with himself, he did it because he knew it would piss Dax off, and he wanted to show him who was in control.

He removed Dona's card from his wallet, dialed the number, and hit the send button. The phone rang only once when he heard, "Dona Powers."

"Hi, Dona, this is Jack, Jack Cameron."

"Hi, Jack."

"Is this a convenient time?" Jack asked.

"Of course," she responded. "We're just about to board our plane back to Portland."

"Oh," Jack said. "I'm sorry, I thought you'd be back home by now."

"Almost," she responded. "We wanted to meet with the other boat captain before we left Skagway," she explained.

Jack felt the blood drain from his face. *Oh shit, I hope I didn't blow this.*

"And how did that go?" Jack asked with as much calm as he could muster.

There was suddenly silence on the other end of the line.

"It's after six o'clock, Jack," Dona said calmly. "You've obviously decided against our offer."

I'll be damned, they're calling my bluff? Jack dug deep to keep his composure, to make the next words count.

"I'm sorry about that," Jack said. "I had to see if I could put together a crew and verify a few things, and to be completely honest, I was undecided until a short time ago."

"And now?" Dona asked.

"I'm in, if you want me," he said. "But I'm still a little uneasy about this."

"What is making you uneasy?" Dona asked.

"With all due respect, it's your brother."

"Why does Dax make you uneasy?" she asked.

"He has a reputation for being extremely difficult, and at this stage in my career, I just don't want the bullshit."

Jack heard Dona take a breath to speak, but he stopped her.

"Please let me finish," Jack said. "I want to make it perfectly clear that the *Lindsey C* is my boat, and I'm her captain. My judgment will not be questioned by you, Dax, or anyone else when it comes to the safety of her or my crew."

Dona sighed. "Fair enough," she said. "Do we have a deal?"

Jack released the breath he hadn't realized he was holding. He'd turned the table again, in his favor. "We have a deal," he said. "When do you want to leave?"

"We'll need to pack the equipment and transport everything to Skagway," Dona explained. "And if all goes as planned, we should be there in three days."

"That should work out just fine," Jack explained. "All we'll need to do is fuel up and load the provisions, and we're good to go."

"Sounds like a plan," Dona said. "I'll be in touch."

"Okay, Dona, thanks."

"Bye-bye, Jack."

Jack hit the end button and immediately dialed Mac and Brad.

MAC and Brad had touched down earlier that afternoon, a little after one o'clock. It had taken the better part of three hours to secure and unload the small plane and pack everything into a four-wheeler to get it up to their mountain retreat. Once up the mountain, it had taken another couple of hours to unload and put everything away.

Mac had dinner on the stove, and Brad had just opened a nice bottle of Pinot Noir, and they were now comfortably sitting on their porch swing, sipping wine and looking out over the pink, orange, and lavender sky as the Alaskan sun dipped just below Mt. McKinley.

They were discussing their new adventure, planning menus and making lists as if the urgency would help speed things along. Their planning was interrupted by the ringing of the cabin's satellite phone. Mac looked at the caller ID and said, "It's Jack."

Mac pressed the "on" button and held the phone loosely to his ear so Brad could lean in and listen as well.

"Hey, Jack."

"It's a go," Jack said. "We leave in three days."

Brad yelled. Mac put his finger in his ear and moved it back and forth in an attempt to stop the ringing sounds. "Okay then," he said. "What time?"

"My charter is due back late morning, and we'll need to fuel up and load the provisions before we can leave again," Jack said. "But I imagine we'll push away either that afternoon or at first light the next morning."

"We'll plan on flying out day after tomorrow, shop for provisions, and be at the dock by noon," Mac said. "Will that work?"

"Sounds like a plan," Jack said. "I'll call you if anything changes."

"Okay—and, Jack?" Mac said.

"Yeah?"

"Thanks, man!"

"My pleasure, it'll be fun," he said.

"See ya, Jack," Mac said as he hung up the phone.

When Mac hung up the satellite phone, Brad was beaming. They discussed their trip a few minutes longer, but it was starting to get a bit nippy. The early summer days were quite mild in the mountains, but the temperatures at night still dipped below freezing, and once the sun had set, they'd decided to make their way inside and light a fire to get the chill out of the cabin.

With the evening chores complete, they were now snuggled up on the couch, finishing a second bottle of Pinot Noir and watching the fire roar in the huge stone fireplace. They were so ready for another adventure, and crewing on Jack's boat, hunting sunken treasure, was just what the doctor ordered.

Brad was lying with his back against Mac's chest, staring into the blazing fire, when he rolled over and looked into Mac's eyes.

"Do you think we'll find the treasure?" Brad asked.

"Who knows," Mac replied. "Dax seems to be the real deal, and supposedly the screwup of the last expedition was just a fluke, so I guess there's a good possibility."

"Wow, we're going to be real-life treasure hunters."

Chapter *3*

IT WAS eleven o'clock that night when Dax Powers pulled into his driveway. Following their day in Skagway, he and Dona had flown back to Portland, and after he'd dropped her off, he'd quickly made his way home. He was thoroughly exhausted, mentally and physically. He'd felt certain when six o'clock had come and gone that Jack had called their bluff of finding or bringing in another boat and decided not to accept their offer.

He'd stripped off his clothing as he made his way to his bedroom and crawled into bed. Unfortunately, as tired as he was, sleep didn't come. He lay in bed, tossing and turning and brooding over the fact that he had to give away two and a half million dollars of his and Dona's possible fortune to some asshole with a charter boat. *I only have myself to blame. If I hadn't lost my boat on that last expedition, we wouldn't be in this position.* It would be at least a year before the new boat would be ready, and he needed this purse to pay for it. The insurance had covered the old boat, but the new state-of-the-art boat, with all the latest reconnaissance equipment, cost three times more than the insurance company had paid him.

He sighed. *It is what it is, and I'll just have to get used to it, but that doesn't mean I have to like it.*

On the flip side of the coin, he'd be lying to himself if he didn't admit the asshole was the most gorgeous thing he'd ever seen. Dax was admittedly a hard-ass who never went for small talk and tried not to mix business with pleasure. Sometimes he was successful and sometimes not so much, but when he first saw Captain Jack standing on the bridge of his boat, he was truly at a loss for words. Jack was a living Adonis, and when he'd smiled at him, he'd felt like he was suddenly under some sort of spell. Damn if he wasn't immediately drawn to the man, and it pissed him off and excited him at the same time. He wasn't there for romance, and the fact that his dick said otherwise really got his blood boiling.

Dax rolled over onto his stomach and punched his pillow. He closed his eyes and immediately saw Jack standing on the bridge. He saw himself walking toward Jack, never breaking eye contact, his strawberry-blond hair reflecting the morning sun's glow brighter than the sun itself. And when he finally got on board, Dax was literally speechless. Jack must have thought he was a complete idiot for not accepting his hand when he'd offered it for a shake. *I'm a hard-ass all right, but I'm not rude.* Jack's crystal-blue eyes were like the most beautiful sapphires he'd ever seen, and that body… not the over-the-top bodybuilder type, but the naturally muscular type that signals discipline and strenuous workouts.

Jack was arrogant as hell, all right, and Dax knew all about being arrogant, but he reminded himself that that's how he got shit done, no matter what people said about him. But at the same time, the smug and confident way Jack had interacted with him and Dona challenged him, and he sure liked a challenge. He was certain Jack was straight, and of course business was business, so he'd have to put his infatuation aside and get the job done. If he didn't get control of himself, Jack would torment him for the entire trip, and Dax prided himself on being the tormentor. He'd need to keep his tough shell intact and keep Jack at a distance, or he would certainly be doomed.

He lay there, trying to put Jack out of his mind. He forced himself to think about how lucky he and Dona had been to stumble on the documents about the *Anna Wyoming*. They had been in the Library of Congress in Washington, DC, further researching the *Sarah Maria* and coming up empty-handed, when he'd opened one last journal, hoping it would contain some new information. But after reading the entire journal, he again came up with nothing. As he was about to close the journal, he spotted the corner of a piece of parchment paper sticking out of what appeared to be a false lining on the back cover of the journal. He gently tugged the page from its cocoon, hoping it was more information about the *Sarah Maria*, but lo and behold, it was not one, but two pages from a wreck called the *Anna Wyoming*. He remembered briefly reading about that wreck a few years back when he was trying to decide on his next expedition, but too little was known, and every attempt to find the wreck had been unsuccessful despite the exact coordinates recorded by eyewitness accounts.

The first of the two pages was actually the last page from the handwritten ship's log, describing the ship's direction and approximate location and that she was taking a pounding and going down in heavy winds and rough seas. The second, much to his delight, was from the chief purser's journal detailing the contents of the purser's safe, which included eight seven-ounce pouches of gold powder, a few pieces of jewelry, and six-thousand-one hundred-and-thirty-two dollars in cash. As a footnote to the inventory of the safe, the journal also eluded to other valuable cargo held in the cargo hold in the center of the ship's hull.

Dax remembered his research, and by all accounts, there were no survivors. But if these records were real, someone must have survived. Dax folded the two pages slowly and slipped them into his pants pocket, then he closed the book and told Dona it was time to go. When they got outside and he was able to tell her what he'd found, she was just as surprised and elated as he was.

That had been four months ago, to the day, and they'd spent every second of that time rereading and researching every detail of the wreck. They further researched the weather conditions of that deadly night, to determine things like which way the winds were blowing and if it was low tide or high tide. The tidal conditions would tell them the direction of the current, which would in turn indicate how far from the original coordinates the ship would have drifted as it went down. The one thing they knew for certain was that the original eyewitness accounts of where the ship went down were nowhere near the location of the wreck, according to these new documents.

No detail was too small, and every bit of information played an important part in the expedition. They had again searched the Internet endlessly and exhausted every journal and newspaper article they could find. They felt like they were as prepared as they could be and were ready to get the expedition started. The most important thing now was to fly under the radar. There is a very small circle of treasure hunters, and they usually kept an eye on one another, hoping to get a scoop or stake a claim on someone else's find.

Dax's mind continued doing backflips. He knew the next few days would prove to be very busy, trying to get their equipment into Skagway harbor unnoticed and then eventually loaded onto the boat. Exhausted, Dax finally shut his mind off and hoped for sleep. His last thought before he drifted off was of the handsome Captain Jackson Cameron.

IN HER bedroom, Donatella lounged on the fainting couch in her favorite silk pajamas, with a copy of *Out* magazine on her lap and a vodka martini straight up with extra olives in her hand. She'd been trying to concentrate on the latest plans for Ellen DeGeneres and Portia de Rossi's wedding, but her mind kept wandering back to the earlier meeting.

As soon as they'd driven up in the taxi and Dax had spotted Jack, Donatella had immediately noticed the gleam in Dax's eyes, and it didn't sit well with her at all. Her twin brother on an expedition was a pain in the ass at best, but he knew his stuff better than anyone she'd ever known. He seemed to be able to sense a wreck by simply floating hundreds of feet above it, and until the *Sarah Maria*, he'd had a hundred-percent success rate. She'd known his pride had been badly wounded when he'd failed at finding the *Sarah Maria* and had lost the *Hunter's Instinct*. She assumed that he was probably looking for a male conquest to get his pride back in shape, but as far as she was concerned, he needed to suck it up, get over it, and get his head back in the game. They needed this purse, and didn't have time for one of Dax's flash-in-the-pan romances to screw things up.

In all their years of treasure hunting, she'd never had an onboard fling or brought any of her girlfriends along on an expedition. Dax, on the other hand, always said that he didn't mix business with pleasure, but he had a very short and convenient memory. *What gives him the right to carry on like a sex-hungry teenager? He's had more onboard romances than a cruise ship gigolo.* Her one consolation was that Jack wasn't normally Dax's type. Jack appeared to be at least thirty-five, and Dax usually liked the young, starry-eyed boys who worshipped him and hung on his every word. And if Dax hadn't already realized that the starry-eyed-boy description clearly didn't fit Jack in any way, shape, or form, he would, soon enough. In fact, she thought that if you took the potential of an affair away from the equation, they just might butt heads, which would create another whole set of problems.

Weighing the two evils—onboard romance or constant conflict— she thought that maybe she should encourage the romance and try to keep Dax happy as long as she could, but she didn't know if Jack was even interested. He looked and acted pretty straight, but her gaydar was telling her otherwise. She would just wait it out and see what happened. Maybe, just once, it would all work out.

She downed the last of her martini and eyed her bed, all dressed in silk linens and awaiting her return. She'd always been considered a lipstick lesbian because she wore makeup, dresses, and high heels. She liked the term, because she really enjoyed being a woman and all the frilly things that came with it. It was such a dichotomy, because while she and Dax were on expeditions, she was as tough as the next guy, always pulling her weight and never needing any special treatment. But when she was at home, it was a totally different story. She decided before she turned in that she would draw a hot bubble bath and soak for a little while, to give the martini time to kick in before she tried to sleep.

As she soaked in the glorious lavender bubbles, she replayed the meeting with Jack in her head. She and Dax had almost blown the deal. In fact, when six o'clock came and went, she'd felt certain that Jack had decided to pass on their offer. The only option she'd had at the time was to bluff about meeting the other boat captain. It was easy enough for him to verify if she'd actually talked to him or not, but she didn't think he'd gone that far. In the end, it all worked out, so there was no sense worrying about it.

Tomorrow would be a very busy day for both of them. Their normal crew had taken temporary jobs while the new boat was being built, so that meant they would have to start packing all their equipment and get it ready for Skagway on their own. Their equipment was a mixture of new and old. Once the weather had cleared in Cape Horn, they'd salvaged most of the equipment from the *Hunter's Instinct* and were able to save some of it, but a great deal of it was ruined and had to be replaced. New equipment always presented problems, which drove Dax crazy, and that in turn drove her crazy. So just for tonight, she would forget the issues at hand and relax, probably for the last time in a long while.

Chapter 4

THE next few days flew by very quickly for everyone. Jack's charter group had departed as planned, and the *Lindsey C* was due back into port by late morning. Mac and Brad had flown in from Hiline Lake by floatplane earlier that morning, rented a truck, and headed into town to buy provisions. And last, but not least, Dax and Dona were making the two-day drive with all their gear loaded in their rental truck. If everything went as planned, everyone would meet at the dock no later than two o'clock, fuel the boat, load the gear and provisions, and cast off by first light the next morning.

Mac and Brad were the first to reach the dock, with enough provisions for two months. They had spent the better part of the last three days putting menus together, making grocery lists, and writing down everything they might need, such as batteries, flashlights, and medical supplies to complete the inventory. If the expedition ran longer than that, they would need to make a trip back to port to restock.

Mac saw the unmarked rental truck first and said, "It looks like we have company."

"I think you're right," Brad said as they both turned and watched the truck pull up to the dock.

Dax and Dona got out of the truck and nervously checked out their surroundings. They slowly made their way to where Mac and Brad were sitting and had started introducing themselves to one another when they saw the *Lindsey C* enter the harbor. *So far so good*, Dona thought.

Jack docked, settled the bill with his charter, and said his good-byes. He walked over to where his crew was standing, hugged Mac and Brad, and shook hands with Dona. He looked at Dax; this time Dax was the first to offer his hand, and Jack accepted it. They all looked at each other with crooked smiles and an unspoken sense of excitement.

Dona finally said, "Let's get moving, gentlemen, we don't have all day."

Everyone took a hand in loading the boat while Mac met the fuel truck he had requested earlier that day. When the boat's main tanks were full, he moved aft to the reserve tanks and filled them as well. It took four hours to get the boat fueled, loaded with provisions, and ready to depart.

"Do you guys want to leave tonight?" Jack asked. "Or would you rather wait until first light?"

They had a lot to discuss, so they decided to wait until the morning. "Let's sit down and discuss the expedition over a cocktail," Dona suggested.

"Perfect," Brad said.

Everyone settled in the salon and started making small talk. Brad and Mac seemed to hit it off with Dax right away.

He's not such a bad guy, Mac thought. *Maybe his reputation is all hype. Time will tell.*

Jack and Dona were pleasant to one another—a little reserved, but cordial. Unfortunately, Jack and Dax were a completely different story. Both men seemed to eye one another from the minute Jack docked the boat. Jack took every opportunity to sneak a peek at Dax and Dax did the same with Jack. Even while everyone was conversing, they seemed to keep their distance and occasionally glare at each other. Jack couldn't figure out why Dax held his attention or why Dax seemed to be keeping an eye on him as well. *The guy runs hot and cold*, Jack thought. *One minute he's shaking my hand and the next he's glaring at me.*

Because they had so much to talk about before they pulled away from the dock the next morning, they all pitched in and made spaghetti, garlic bread, and a salad and decided to have a working dinner. Dax spoke first to explain the mission.

"On the afternoon of February 5th, 1898," he said, "the *Anna Wyoming* entered the Lynn Canal, heading for Skagway from an unknown destination with an unknown number of passengers. The Lynn Canal is not really a canal, but more of an inlet that runs ninety miles from the inlets of the Chilkat River south to Chatham Straight and Stephens Passage. The most reliable reports put the number of passengers between twenty-five and forty, although accounts written years later inflate that figure to as many as one hundred fifty. It was said that most of the passengers were transporting large amounts of gold, but until now, that was just a theory. Within a few hours, a heavy wind developed from the north. Various observers on land estimated the winds at fifty to eighty miles per hour, with the higher figures more common. I'm sure Jack can speak to this more thoroughly than I can, but I'm told that during a northerly blow, the mountains alongside the Lynn Canal form a long tunnel that can substantially increase the force of the wind."

Jack nodded his head in agreement.

Dax continued. "Sometime during the night, the southbound steamer struck an uncharted, submerged pinnacle a few hundred yards north of Eldred Rock. Newspaper accounts report a flash seen from the shore some eight miles away. These reports may not be reliable, but they did fuel speculation about the nature of the wreck. According to official accounts, no one survived the wreck. Given the high winds and waves, the steep and sharp outcropping of nearby Eldred Rock, and the icy weather, survival would have been a miracle. Despite these facts, rumors and circumstantial evidence have given rise to a popular theory that the vessel was wrecked on purpose as a cover-up for an attempt to steal the large amounts of gold hidden on board. If true, this would make the wreck of the *Anna Wyoming* the greatest mass murder in Alaskan history."

Everyone was on the edge of their seat, especially Brad and Mac. They wanted an adventure, and by God, an adventure was what they were getting. Brad couldn't contain himself any longer. "I'm so excited, I think I'm peeing down both legs," he said with a grin. That broke the ice, and everyone, including Dax, had to chuckle at that. Mac nudged and shushed him and motioned for Dax to continue.

He next explained that they would start the search at the actual coordinates the captain had recorded just before the ship went down, which were very different from the eyewitness accounts, and work their way further south from there. It would be endless days of crawling along at idle speeds up and down, back and forth along imaginary grids, stopping only to mark a potential spot for a reconnaissance dive. He handed Jack the general coordinates and asked him to chart the imaginary grid and commit to navigating it as closely as possible. This would allow the sonar to do its job and cover every inch of the target area.

Dona spoke next. They would all work together during the day, but at night they would work four-hour shifts to make sure every station was covered. She began to outline their responsibilities. Since she and Dax had the most experience identifying structures that would indicate a possible wreck site, they would share responsibility for monitoring the sonar equipment. Jack, along with Dax and Dona, were the most-trained divers, so they would share responsibility for reconnaissance dives. Since Brad and Mac were certified divers, after their crew responsibilities they would be in charge of maintaining the dive equipment and assisting on dives when needed. Mac, being a pilot, would also share responsibility for captaining the boat when Jack was taking his four-hour break, and Brad would act as a floater wherever he was needed.

By the time dinner was over, everyone knew their role and felt energized to be part of the expedition—everyone except Jack. He knew he was being petty and that this was Dax's expedition, but he wasn't happy that Dax was running the show on his boat. He decided that he would roll with it for now, but if Dax continued to treat him like crew on his own boat, he would put his foot down.

After dinner and briefing, everyone helped clean the galley and talked about turning in early. Jack took the lead and retired to his master cabin. Mac and Brad took the V-berth, and Dax and Dona each had their own cabin next to one another. They would use the fourth crew berth as home base, and set up all the equipment in the smaller cabin.

Jack sat at the tiny desk in his cabin, toed off his deck shoes, and for the next thirty minutes listened to the comings and goings of everyone getting settled in their cabins. Eventually, the crew settled down, and all he heard were the gentle waves lapping along the hull and the slight whistle of the breeze through his cabin porthole.

He started to review the navigational charts and the coordinates Dax had given him, and he found his mind wandering. *Dax Powers, what an ass. The man sure has a lot of nerve. Yeah, he'd chartered my boat, but he hasn't spent a penny. Mac and Brad and I are sharing the cost of fuel and provisions, and if we find nothing, together we'll be out half the expenses. Maybe I was too hasty and should have passed on this charter.*

But then a gleam entered his eye. *On the other hand, what if we do find the wreck, and what if there is ten million dollars worth of gold on board? I'll have a couple million dollars in my pocket after I cover expenses and pay Mac and Brad. I can certainly live with that.*

He stared at the charts, not really paying attention. He just couldn't stop thinking about Dax and Dona. What was it about Dax that rubbed him the wrong way? Why was he so fixated on him? Jack didn't know the answer, but he knew there was something that just didn't sit right with him. Dona, on the other hand, was an impressive woman, and a looker too. She technically knew her stuff, but his mind wandered back to Dax. It was very clear that Dax had the passion for treasure hunting, by the way his eyes lit up when he talked about every minute detail of the wreck.

Jack shook his head to try and clear his mind. He forced himself to focus on the charts and finally charted their course from the coordinates Dax had given him. First thing in the morning, he would plug the coordinates into the Global Satellite Positioning, or GPS, computer, and that in turn would allow the autopilot to track the course without the need of paper charts. *Enough for one day*, he thought. He pushed away from his little desk and turned off his desk lamp. He undressed, hit the head, and then climbed into his bunk. He tossed and turned, unable to sleep. He started to think about Dona in the cabin next door. He pictured her tall, graceful frame slowly undressing and sliding into bed. His dick started to take notice of his fantasy. He reached over to the nightstand drawer and removed a small bottle of lotion. *This will do the trick*, he thought as he squeezed the smooth liquid into his hand and started rubbing his already-hard cock. He pictured Dona lying next to him and kissing every inch of his body from head to toe. He then pictured her straddling him and lowering herself onto him. He gasped when his cock entered her smooth, velvety tunnel. As she rode him, in his mind, his hand moved faster and faster. He felt that all-too-familiar release about to explode as his balls drew up inside him. As the first shot of his warm load landed on his chest, he closed his eyes and, much to his dismay, it wasn't Dona's face he saw, but Dax's.

"What the fuck," he whispered. He didn't even acknowledge the second and third shots as they hit his chest. "Now the guy is tormenting me in my fantasies."

FIRST light came, with the crew chomping at the bit to get started. Jack, in a piss-poor mood with not much sleep, had hit the bridge at five o'clock that morning to check the weather report and program the GPS. Still preoccupied with the previous night's fantasy cluster-fuck, he fired up his engines as the rest of the crew tended to the lines and fenders. He sounded two whistle blows to signal their departure as he maneuvered the boat away from the dock. Everyone was so excited and preoccupied with their assigned jobs that no one noticed the man sitting in the black Mercedes sedan with binoculars, studying them as they made their way out of port.

The *Lindsey C*'s dark hull smoothly parted the waters of the Lynn Canal while Jack started to prepare his search grid. *Damn if I'm going to look like an amateur to Dax. After all, I was captaining a boat when he was just starting to wear Pull-Ups. Well, probably not. I'm thirty-six, and he doesn't appear to be much older than twenty-nine or thirty.* Then the thought of Dax in Pull-Ups made him smile.

Dax was about to enter the bridge when he stopped short in his tracks. Jack was sitting in his captain's seat, fiddling with the GPS unit and wearing the most beautiful smile he'd ever seen on a man's face. It took everything he had not to walk up behind him, throw his arms around Jack's waist, and hold on for dear life. But Dax knew he had to keep his distance and keep Jack hating him, or he'd never survive this expedition. The minute Jack warmed up to him, he'd be a goner. Dax stood up straight, wiped the smile off of his face, and walked onto the bridge.

"What are you smiling about?" he asked.

Startled out of his thoughts, Jack looked at Dax, blushed, and said, "You really don't want to know."

"Try me," Dax replied.

"Nah, I think I'll pass," Jack said. "But thanks for asking."

"Suit yourself," Dax said. "Are you through with the grid?"

"I've got our first few days completed, based on your coordinates, and will have a fifty-mile block finished by the end of the day tomorrow."

"Jack, I need those by the end of the day," Dax said.

Jack took a deep breath, about to give Dax a piece of his mind, but before he could speak, Dax said, "Now, can this tub go any faster?"

Jack felt the heat rise up into his face. "Why, you little prick," he said. "Let me remind you that this is *my* boat and *I'm* the captain. I don't care how you ran your boat, but on my boat, I set the speed and I decide when we move and when we stop. Got it? Now get off *my* bridge," he said, with an emphasis on "my."

"Well, aren't you an arrogant piece of shit?" Dax snapped. "Who do you think is paying for this charter?"

"Certainly not you," Jack barked back. "Unless, of course, you're paying in insults, because otherwise I haven't seen a dime from you." Jack paused and held his breath for a second to calm down, and then he continued. "Every dime spent to get this boat ready has come from me. Sure, we have a contract, but based on your recent fuck-up, it may not be worth the paper it's written on. Now what part of *get off my bridge* did you not understand?"

For a second Jack thought he recognized a hurt look on Dax's face. But just as quickly as the look came, it disappeared, leaving nothing but anger in his hazel-colored eyes.

Dax turned to leave the bridge, stopped, and looked back. "You'll get your money, Jack. By God, if it kills me, you'll get your fucking money."

They reached the strike zone, and Jack idled the engines while Dona and Dax, with the help of Mac and Brad, carefully lowered the sonar equipment into the water. Dona had spent the time underway in the crew berth, setting up the sonar receiver and the receiver for the *Hunter II*, which was the unmanned remotely operated vehicle (ROV), which would transmit pictures from below the surface should they need to investigate a particular site. Earlier that morning she'd wired the bridge directly to the crew berth so they could communicate privately, without broadcasting highly classified information over a two-way radio.

With the sonar equipment safely underwater, she made her way down to the crew berth to join Dax. She flipped on the radio and pressed the transmit button.

"Base to bridge, Jack do you read?"

"Loud and clear, Dona," Jack responded.

"Perfect," she said. "Sonar is loaded and ready to go."

"Roger that," Jack said as he put the boat in gear.

The *Lindsey C* began to slowly inch forward.

"What speed would you like to maintain?" Jack asked.

"Let's try and keep her between five to seven knots, and see how it goes."

"Roger that."

Jack engaged the autopilot and sat back to see how his boat responded to his charted course. The first few turns were fairly quick and tight because of the sheer confinements of the grid, but the maneuvers got wider with each pass, and things quickly evened out. In a very short time, the *Lindsey C* was steadily creeping along, approaching each waypoint, then changing course and heading to the next. If Dona or Dax saw anything interesting on the sonar, they would radio the bridge to idle the engines, get the exact coordinates, and do a print screen of the computer monitor to record the coordinates and proceed again.

As Dax and Dona sat in the dark quiet of the crew cabin with only the glow from the computer screens, Dax used his time to decide how to divide the crew into shifts. He'd not seen Jack since he'd stormed off the bridge that morning and knew Jack was doing his best to avoid him. He normally didn't care if he was disliked, and was especially happy when people avoided him, but Jack avoiding him, although he knew it was probably for the best, really rubbed him the wrong way. *If he thinks he can avoid me, I'll show him.*

Dax assigned Dona and Mac shift one, which left him and Jack to share the second shift. *This'll really piss him off,* Dax thought. Since Brad had little to do besides his crew chores until they actually started diving, Dax assigned him the job of floating between base and the bridge, checking on Mac and Dona and getting them anything they might need. Everyone would work four hours on and four hours off. *That'll give me four hours to torment Jack into really hating me.* And that thought saddened him, but he knew it was for the best.

When Mac took a copy of the shift schedule to the bridge, he knew it would be the straw that broke the camel's back. And he was right; Jack was as pissed off as Mac had ever seen him. "That son of a bitch is determined to taunt me, day in and day out," Jack yelled. "But not anymore. Take the helm, Mac."

In a huff, Jack stormed off the bridge on a direct route to home base. He turned the corner into the crew berth and ran smack into Brad, who was on his way out of the small space. Brad saw the look in Jack's eyes, and having seen that look a time or two in his day, knew what it meant and got out of his way. Dax and Dona were staring at the computer monitor. Dax looked up with a slight grin on his face, and said, "Hey, Jack."

Dax studied Jack, standing in the companionway door and looking as good as any man ever had. His hands were at his sides, clenched tightly into fists, and his face was as red as a Coca-Cola can. *Sexy as hell.*

"Don't *hey, Jack* me, you son of a bitch. I've taken just about enough of your bullshit on my boat as I'm gonna take. Who the hell do you think you are?"

Dax continued to stare at Jack in the doorway. *Damn, he looks hot when he's angry.*

"What's blown up your skirt, Jack?" he asked in a very calm voice, all the while still grinning.

"Don't act innocent with me, you arrogant piece of shit. You know what's *blown up my skirt*, as you call it. Lots of things have *blown up my skirt* since you boarded *my boat*, but why in the hell would you schedule us to work together when it's pretty obvious we hate each other?"

"Why, Jack, I don't hate you, and I'm deeply crushed to learn that you hate me. What have I ever done to you?"

"For starters, you've done nothing but taunt and disrespect me on my own boat since you first stepped out of the taxi at the dock. You wouldn't speak to me. You wouldn't have shaken my hand if Dona hadn't broken a rib to make you do it. And you try to tell me what to do at every turn. You're a socially inept ass is what you are, Dax," Jack continued.

That statement confirmed Dax's fears that Jack had taken his stunned silence and inability to move as an arrogant gesture instead of realizing it was because he was so intimidated by his good looks.

He snapped out of his thoughts when Jack slammed his fist into the cabin door.

"The way I see it," he said, "you have a pretty shitty way of treating someone you can't do without."

That did it. Dax didn't care how hot Jack was, he had just crossed the line. He jumped up and stood chest to chest with Jack. Jack's eyes widened, but he held his ground.

"You think we can't do this without you, Captain Jackson P. Cameron?" Dax asked.

"Damn straight," Jack shot back.

"Then you're delusional," Dax yelled. "I don't need you or this two-bit bathtub. And by the way, does the P in your name stand for 'prick'?"

Suddenly everything went into slow motion. He saw Jack slowly draw his fist back and heard the slurred words, "W-h-y y-o-u s-o-r-r-y p-i-e-c-e o-f...." Something came over Dax, and at that moment, all he saw were Jack's crystal-blue eyes shining with anger; his shoulders, broad and strong; and that fist, that beautiful fist coming right at his face. He fought the urge, tooth and nail, but surprised even himself when he leaned in and cupped Jack on the back of the neck to draw him in as he crushed his lips against Jack's. Brad's eyes widened, and silence filled the tiny cabin.

Dona slammed her fist on the table and yelled, "Enough! Get a grip, you two."

Dax broke the kiss and stepped away from Jack. Jack, stunned, dropped his fist down to his side. He wiped his red, swollen lips, and all he could think to say was "Peyton, my middle name is Peyton." But other than that, he was at a total loss.

Dona continued. "I think I speak for everyone when I say we've all had just about enough of your lovers' quarrels. You boys either act on your high-school man crushes or get the fuck over them. I don't care who has the biggest dick, but we're going to finish this expedition in one piece, and you're gonna damn well like it."

"Lovers' quarrels? Man crushes?" Jack screamed. "What are you talking about—we're not even gay."

A small curve developed on Dax's lips. "Speak for yourself, Captain. I thought everyone knew I was gay."

Jack turned around and looked at Brad, who was standing outside the cabin door with a grin on his face. Brad nodded, and Jack looked hurt and defeated. He looked at Dona, then Dax, and turned and walked out of the cabin.

"I think that went better than planned," Dax said with a chuckle.

"Dax, you shouldn't have kissed him. If he ends this expedition, we're screwed. You get your shit together and figure out a way to make nice with Jack, and get him to change his mind, because despite what you think, we *do* need him and his boat."

"Yes, ma'am," Dax said with a military salute.

JACK stood in the hallway for a few seconds, trying to absorb what had just happened. *Dax is gay, and Brad and Mac didn't think it was important enough to tell me. The guy just kissed me right in front of everyone. Who does he think he is?*

He turned around and walked right back into the cabin. He looked at Dona and said, in a very even, calm voice, "I think this was a mistake. I'll absorb the expenses thus far, and I'll chalk it up to a learning experience." He rubbed his still-swollen lips again and looked at Dax. "A real learning experience. I'll get you guys back to the dock at first light."

"Jack, don't make any rash decisions," Dona gently pleaded. "Dax and I have our hearts and souls tied up in this expedition, not to mention we all have money invested. We are so close, I can feel it."

Dax and Brad stood motionless, not knowing what to say or do. Jack looked around the room, at Dax and Dona and then at Brad.

"All this drama," Jack said as he lifted his hands and gestured to them all, "is not worth it to me. Dax and I are who we are, probably more alike than I care to admit, but that's certainly not going to change. And… my friends, I guess I'm a joke to them."

Brad opened his mouth, but Jack put his hand up to stop him. "I don't want to hear it. I hope you've all enjoyed your fun at my expense, but it stops here."

JACK sheepishly made his way topside, with Brad on his heels. When he reached the bridge, Mac saw the expression on Jack's face and looked at Brad.

"What did I miss?" he whispered to Brad.

Jack took the captain's chair next to Mac, and Brad moved over and stood next to Mac's seat.

"The jig is up," Jack said to Mac.

"What do you mean, the jig is up?" Mac asked.

"The fact that neither of you found the need to tell me that Dax was gay," he said.

Mac looked over at Brad and grinned.

Jack continued, "How was that little tidbit of information overlooked in that novel of a story you told me over the phone when I asked if you'd ever heard of Dax Powers?"

"I didn't think it was relevant," Mac responded. "I know how you feel about gay people."

"Come on, man, not that again. Damn it, guys! Are we ever going to get past this?" Jack asked. "Yes, I made a mistake, and yes, you guys almost lost each other over my mistake, but I've apologized for it over and over again. What more can I do?"

"There's nothing you can do, Jack." Mac looked at Brad then back to Jack. "What happened down there anyway?"

"Well," Jack said, "one minute I was giving Dax a piece of my mind, then the next, he was kissing me."

Mac's face morphed into a grin, and he looked at Brad. Brad nodded in agreement, and they both high-fived.

"What are you two high-fiving about?" Jack asked. "Is that why you didn't tell me Dax was gay? Are you trying to convert me?"

Mac took the lead. "Very funny, Jack. We can't convert anyone who isn't remotely interested, but really, what does it matter if Dax is gay or not?"

"If it didn't matter, why didn't you just tell me?"

"Because we thought that, if you knew, you might not take the charter," Mac said. "And we've been waiting for you to come out of the closet on your own and thought this might help."

"Oh," Jack said. Then Mac's words registered. "What?" he yelled.

"Think about it, Jack. One very short marriage many years ago. No lasting relationships. Hell, you haven't even had a date in years, not to mention that fact that you're so homophobic."

"What, now you think I'm homophobic?" Jack asked.

Brad jumped in this time. "We've always thought that, Jack. You remember how you reacted when you found out Mac and I were involved. Do you not remember the fight in our living room? Demanding to be flown back to Anchorage, making Mac choose between me and his family? Come on, Jack, your memory's not that bad."

For the second time that day, Jack looked totally defeated. "I remember everything," he said. "I was just scared, I guess."

"Look," Mac said. "It happens to the best of us." Mac reached over and grabbed Brad's hand. "Brad and I didn't plan on falling in love. In fact, it was the last thing either of us expected. He was still struggling with Jeff's death, and I was a straight man, still mourning the loss of my wife six years after her death, but it happened. Luckily, we were able to recognize the love that grew between us and allow ourselves to be happy. And to tell you the truth, I've never looked back. I loved Lindsey with all my heart, but Lindsey's gone, and that relationship died when we buried her. Do you remember how hard it was for me?"

Jack nodded in agreement.

"But now, I love Brad, and we've made a damn good life for ourselves. I didn't think I was gay, and I'd never even looked at a man in a sexual way, but the heart wants what it wants, Jack. Just think about what I've said, and don't worry about labels right now."

"Did the kiss gross you out?" Brad asked.

"Yes! No! I don't know," Jack replied with a very confused look. "Why are we even having this conversation?" he asked. "I'm not gay."

"Fine," Mac said. "You're not gay, but we are what we are, whether we label ourselves or not. Just please promise me that you'll keep an open mind, and do what feels right."

"It doesn't really matter anyway, the expedition is over, and Dax will go his way, and I'll go mine. We're heading back to port at first light."

"What?" Mac said. "Are you serious? Can't you and Dax get past this and work together?"

"I doubt it," Jack said.

"Just think about everything we said and don't make any decisions until morning, okay?"

Jack seemed to be listening, but didn't respond. He looked down at his watch. "Ten o'clock," he said. "You guys take a break, and I'll see you at two o'clock."

Mac stood and gave Jack a hug. Brad laid his hand on Jack's arm and said, "If you need anything, or if you just need to talk, give either of us a call."

"Thanks, guys," Jack said. "But I'll be fine, see you at two."

Brad and Mac left the bridge, and Jack climbed into the captain's chair and checked his equipment. Everything was going as planned—except for Dax, of course. Just an hour ago, he had been about to knock Dax on his ass, and in the heat of that moment, Dax had kissed him. Jack reached up and touched his lips to try and remember the feeling.

He settled back in his chair and closed his eyes. If he was going to be honest with himself—and it was high time he was—he had liked it. It had been hot and manly, and when their five o'clock shadows brushed against one another, he'd felt a spark. It was sexy as hell, and he was pretty sure he wanted to do it again.

The whole "gay" thing threw him, though. He didn't think he was gay. In all of his years, he'd never even experimented with a guy, like most adolescent boys did. He tried to think back over his life to see if he could ever remember being attracted to a guy, and damn if Dax didn't quickly enter his mind. *Other than Dax, you idiot.* The sight of Dax's hazel-colored eyes, right before they kissed, came into his mind. The heat was incredible, and there was definitely something there. *Did Dax feel it too?* He shook his head from side to side in an attempt to get Dax out of his mind's eye and tried to focus on his thoughts again.

Yeah, he'd noticed a good-looking guy once or twice. Sometimes when he watched porn, he would occasionally catch himself looking at the guy as much as the girl, but that didn't make him gay, did it? Then he thought about how Mac and Brad had found each other. He'd never quite understood how Mac could be straight one day and gay the next, but again, Mac didn't believe in labels. Shortly after he'd found out about Mac and Brad, he remembered Mac trying to explain that he thought people were attracted to who they were attracted to. It didn't matter if it was a woman or a man, but society dictates who you should and shouldn't love. Mac and Brad, gay or straight, seem to be genuinely happy in their relationship. He racked his brains. Why had he had such a hard time with Mac and Brad?

Did Mac and Brad falling in love hit too close to home for me, and that's why I was so against it? Had I pushed my desires for men so far to the back of my mind that I didn't even realize I was gay? The funny thing was that the thought of them having sex didn't gross him out or anything, so what was it? Maybe the reality that two men could fall in love was just too much for him to handle. If they could do it and be happy and so in love, then maybe he could too, and that would mean he would have to face up to the fact that he might be gay. Boy, did that scare the hell out of him.

His thoughts were all over the place, and he was no longer making sense, so he tried to boil it all down into something he could digest. *Okay, I'm attracted to Dax. No labels yet. One day at a time.*

Dax's voice suddenly filled the bridge.

"Base to bridge, Jack, do you copy?"

"Bridge here," he responded.

"Look, Jack, call me a coward, but I thought it would be easier if I did this over the radio."

"I'm listening," Jack said.

Dax hesitated for about ten seconds, and Jack thought the silence felt like one hundred pounds sitting on his chest.

"I'm sorry, man," Dax finally spit out.

Silence again.

"Sorry for...?" Jack asked.

"Okay, I see you're not going to make this easy for me," Dax whined.

"You were saying...." Jack said.

"Fine, I'm sorry for disrespecting your position as captain. I'm sorry for continually taunting you and trying to ruffle your feathers. And mostly, I'm sorry for being a complete ass. This is no excuse, but I'm really attracted to you, man. I know you're straight and the thought of working so closely with you and not being able to have you was driving me crazy. So I thought that if I pissed you off enough, you'd hate me, and I wouldn't have to worry about controlling my libido around you."

Before Jack could respond, Dax said, "But Jack... let me make one thing very clear."

"I'm listening," Jack said.

"I'm not the least bit sorry for kissing you. Again, I realize you're probably straight, but that part of the fight was really hot."

Jack smiled.

"And besides," Dax said. "It was either kiss you or take a fist to the jaw. And with a face like mine, I always go for the kiss."

Jack realized that, for the first time since they had met, they finally agreed on something.

"Apology accepted," Jack said. "And for the record, I don't regret the kiss, either."

Jack could feel Dax smiling through the radio.

"What?" Dax asked. "Are you gay?"

"I have no idea what I am," Jack said. "I never thought about it before. It was my first kiss from a guy, and I was totally caught off guard, but I kind of liked it."

"Me too," Dax whispered. "So what do we do now?"

"You're asking me?" Jack said. "I have no idea. I'm new to all this."

"Leave the driving to me, and sit back and enjoy the ride, so to speak," Dax said.

"Hold on a minute, Dax," Jack said. "I don't know what to do about all this. Hell, I don't even know if I want to see where this goes."

As soon as Jack said the words, he realized that the thought of experimenting with Dax scared the hell out of him and excited him all at the same time.

"But if I do," he continued, "I'm sure you've realized by now that I'm not the *sit back and enjoy the ride* type of guy. I usually do the driving."

"No problem, we can take turns driving," Dax said with a chuckle.

"Are we talking about what I think we're talking about?" Jack asked.

"Maybe, maybe not," Dax replied.

"Now, you're just teasing me," Jack said.

"How about I come to your cabin when our shift is over and try to persuade you to not cancel the expedition?"

Dax couldn't see the changed expression on Jack's face, but suddenly Jack's already-fragile ego took a hit, and he fell silent. When he finally spoke, his voice was full of disappointment. "Is that what this is all about?" he asked. "Not canceling the expedition?"

"Oh God, no, Jack. I didn't mean that. I mean, sure, I don't want you to cancel the expedition, but it's more than that. I'm really attracted to you."

Jack smiled again, not knowing whether to believe him or not, but one thing was certain. If he did this, there would be no turning back. If he did decide to not cancel the expedition, they were going to be together on this boat, in very tight quarters, for up to three months, and if this didn't work out, it could be the longest three months of his life.

Before he knew what he was doing, he heard the words escape his mouth. "Okay, see you at two." Then he added, "But Dax… we need to take this very slowly."

Dax whispered, "See you at two. Base out."

"Bridge out."

Chapter 5

BRAD and Mac crawled into their bunk, but were not really sleepy. Mac started asking questions about the "incident," which is what they'd dubbed it, and Brad recounted the entire story to him.

"Mac, I wish you could have been there to see the look on Jack's face when Dax kissed him," Brad said. "My God, it was priceless."

Mac smiled. "I always miss the good stuff."

"They both said some pretty horrible things to one another, and Jack was just winding up to cold-cock Dax in the jaw, when Dax reached his hand behind Jack's neck, pulled him in, and planted a big, wet kiss right on Jack's lips."

"It appears that our Dax has some real balls," Mac said.

"I'll say. But wait, it gets better," Brad continued. "Dona slammed her fist on the table and told them to get a grip. That broke the kiss and startled all of us. She told them to get over their high-school man crushes and get on with this expedition."

"She sounds like she has a pair as well," Mac chuckled. "Maybe it runs in the family."

"It appears that she can be tough when she needs to be," Brad said. "Anyway, then Jack denied being gay and waited for Dax to do the same, and when the proclamation never came and Jack realized what that meant, you should have seen the look on his face. Worth every ounce of gold we might find."

"What did Jack do then?" Mac asked.

"He said the expedition wasn't working for him, and he was done. Then he bolted, with me on his heels, and that's when we ended up on the bridge."

"Wow, old Jackie boy with a guy. Are we going to have fun with this or what?" Mac said through a mischievous smile.

"You've got to take it easy on Jack for a while," Brad said. "Let them sort this out for themselves, and once they do, *then* we can give him hell."

"Okay, okay, I hear ya," Mac said. "But he didn't give us time to sort through *our* feelings, and I almost lost you over it."

"You never even came close to losing me," Brad said. "Jack was just a bump in the road, and thanks to him we found out that our bond was truly unbreakable."

Mac gently kissed Brad on the lips. "We have another three hours before we have to be on deck, so what do you think about reinforcing our bond?"

"I thought you'd never ask, flyboy," Brad said as he pulled the covers up over their heads.

IT WAS 1:55 in the morning when Brad and Mac stepped onto the bridge, unnoticed by Jack.

"Shift's over," Mac said.

Deep in thought, Jack was startled back into reality. "Wow, is it two a.m. already?"

"Almost," Brad said.

"Go get some rest, Jack," Mac said.

"I'm not sure about that," Jack replied. "Dax is coming by my cabin to talk."

"Talk, huh?" Brad said with a sly smile.

"Yes, talk," Jack repeated. "I told him that whatever this thing is, it needs to go really slowly."

"Well, what are you doing talking to us? Get down to your cabin, and slip into something more comfortable," Mac joked.

"Very funny, Mac. Are you guys ever gonna let me live this down?" Jack asked.

"Probably not, but we'll take it easy on you for awhile, just until you get used to the idea."

"Thanks a lot," he replied.

"Now get down to your cabin and cross over to the *Dark Side*," Brad said as he winked at Mac. Jack looked at Brad with both fear and amusement, and simply shook his head as he stepped off the bridge.

Jack was still smiling about the *Dark Side* comment as he made his way from the bridge down to the master cabin. When he rounded the stairs, he stopped dead in his tracks, and all thoughts of the *Dark Side* melted away. Dax was casually leaning on the wall opposite his cabin door, smiling broadly. His legs were crossed at the ankle, and his muscular arms were folded across his firm swimmer's chest. Jack felt a flurry of nerves well up inside him, and he was suddenly flushed with embarrassment.

"Anyone ever tell you how hot you are when you're nervous?" Dax asked.

"Not that I can remember," Jack said as he fidgeted like a ten-year-old that had just gotten caught with his hand in the cookie jar.

"Are you going to stand there and fidget all night or are you going to ask me in?" Dax asked with a smirk.

"I haven't decided yet," Jack said as he stepped past Dax and opened the cabin door.

Dax held his ground. "Okay, you can come in," Jack said. "Sorry the place is such a mess, but obviously I didn't know I was going to have a gentlemen caller."

"No problem," Dax said.

Jack watched in silence as Dax kicked off his shoes, and as his tall frame gracefully crawled across the bed. Then Dax flipped over and sat with his back resting against the wall. He smiled and patted the spot next to him.

"What part of 'taking it slow' did you not get?" Jack asked through a smile.

"Look," Dax said, pointing down to the bed. "I'm totally dressed and on top of the covers."

Jack sighed in defeat as he toed off his shoes and hesitantly climbed into the queen-sized berth and sat, shoulder to shoulder, next to Dax.

Jack nervously looked straight ahead and noticed that Dax's legs were at least six inches longer than his own and hung off the end of the berth. His feet were at least two sizes larger too. *This man is big all over*, he thought, and he blushed again when he thought about the implications of that statement.

"That's better," Dax said as he grabbed Jack's hand. "I agreed to take things slowly, but that doesn't mean we can't court," he said with a smile and a wink. Dax was an impatient man, and figured if he didn't push Jack's limits a little every time they were together, he would get nowhere.

Jack glanced down at his hand entwined in another man's hand and swallowed the lump in his throat. He looked back up, and they both sat there, staring ahead and holding hands like a couple of high school kids.

"So, when did you know you were gay?" Dax asked.

"I don't know that I *am* gay," Jack responded.

"Okay, let's work through this," Dax continued. "You're sitting in bed with a gay man who's holding your hand and about to kiss you, and you don't think you're gay?"

Jack opened his mouth to protest, but before he could answer, Dax leaned in and gently kissed him on his full, beautiful lips, then leaned back to his side of the bed.

Stunned, Jack didn't move.

"Were you about to say something?" Dax asked through a smile.

Jack was silent. No matter how hard he tried, he couldn't remember what he was going to say. But besides his inability to speak, he hated the fact that Dax knew he'd kissed the words right out of him.

"Let's try another route," Dax suggested. "When did you know you were attracted to me?"

Jack turned his head to face Dax. "I don't know the answer to that, either," he said shyly. "One minute I was loathing you and the next you were kissing me. That kind of emotional juxtaposition takes a little getting used to, if you know what I mean."

"So, just to make sure I got this right and I'm not barking up the wrong tree," Dax said. "Does Captain Cameron like being kissed by men?"

"I haven't kissed any men," Jack said nervously. "Just you."

"Thanks a lot," Dax responded, his bruised ego very evident in his tone.

"No, that didn't come out right," Jack confessed. "I mean I've never been kissed by any other man *except* you."

"That's better, I think," Dax said as he turned to face Jack.

Jack held up his index finger and said, "But just to set the record straight, I don't want to be kissed by any other man except you."

"Music to my ears," Dax said, as he squeezed Jack's hand.

"Have you always knows you were gay?" Jack asked.

"I've always known, and Dona says the same thing."

"Dona's gay too?" Jack asked.

"Yeah, it's not that uncommon if one twin is gay for the other to be gay too," Dax said.

"If that's not proof that being gay is genetics and not a choice, I don't know what is," Jack professed.

"I know, right," Dax said.

Jack had a million questions rolling around in his head. "How was it, growing up being gay?" he asked. "Were you teased a lot in school?"

"When we were younger we didn't know we were different," Dax said. "Our parents homeschooled us until we went to college, so luckily we never had to endure any of the teasing and bullying you hear so much about these days. Those poor kids," he added.

"Obviously it hasn't affected your adult lives or the way you run your business. Or has it?" Jack asked.

"Don't get me wrong, Jack, sometimes it's been tough," Dax confessed. "I think more so for Dona, being a gay woman in a predominantly male-dominated business, but we try not to take it personally. Some people are just bigots, and that's never going to change."

"Is it tough to get people to take you seriously?" Jack asked.

"As a matter of fact, sometimes we've been able to use the gay thing to our advantage," Dax explained. "Because we're gay, people underestimate us, and that always gives us the upper hand. I have a Masters Degree in Archeology and Dona a Masters in History. We worked our way up by crewing on every expedition we could find and learning everything we could possibly learn from anyone who would teach us. And yeah, I earned a reputation of being a real asshole, but not because I started out that way. We've had to work harder than anyone else to achieve the same results—because we're gay, and because Dona's a woman. This is a straight man's business, and they never let us forget it."

Jack nodded but didn't say anything, not wanting to interrupt Dax's story.

"We mostly work with two types of people. The first type is your typical homophobe who writes us off because we're stupid homosexuals, and how much could we really know about treasure hunting and salvaging? And as I said, we use that to our advantage. That is, until I've had enough of playing their game, and then the real asshole in me comes out, and I quickly live up to my reputation."

"And the second type?" Jack asked.

"The second type is the worst. They pretend to accept us as equals, but do everything to undermine our operation, and stab us in the back at every turn. At least with the homophobes we always know where we stand, and there's some comfort in that, but with these guys, you never know who to trust, so you trust no one."

"I imagine that's tough," Jack confessed. "Always having to look over your shoulder."

"It is," Dax said. "But I earned my reputation because I don't put up with any bullshit, and I do things my way. If I'm wrong, I take the hit, but thankfully, because I do my homework, and I know my shit, I'm normally right on."

Jack was developing a newfound respect for Dax and Dona. Their chosen career wasn't always easy, but they'd kept on course and made their way in the world, and he admired that.

"This is all very enlightening," Jack said. "But make no mistake about it, my disliking you had nothing to do with your being gay. I really had no idea, but apparently Brad and Mac did and never bothered to tell me."

"It's okay, Jack, we get the same shit all the time," Dax said. "We're very used to it."

"I really wasn't playing games with you, Dax," Jack said. "It looked like you were challenging me to a pissing contest at every turn, and I never shy away from a challenge. But again, my issues had nothing to do with whether you and Dona were gay or straight."

"I believe you," Dax said.

"So, based on the two types of people you work with," Jack asked, "where do I fit in?"

Dax thought for a second. "You sort of fall into a new category."

"What category is that?" Jack asked.

"Someone who doesn't care about our sexuality, but is a bit of a control freak, whether he knows it or not, and doesn't want anyone threatening his position."

Jack considered the answer. "Maybe you're half right," he said.

"How so?" Dax asked.

"Don't confuse control with respect. I never once thought I knew more about your expedition than you did, I just know my boat, and I know her limits. And, for the record, I don't want control, I want respect. In any other environment, I have no problem earning someone's respect, but on my boat, I'm captain, no questions asked, end of story," Jack said.

"I get that now," Dax admitted. "And I'm sorry I didn't get it earlier. I'm just so used to captaining my own boat or dealing with assholes that I assumed you were just another one among the many. I was wrong."

"Thanks, Dax, that means a lot," Jack said. "But I think we need to table this discussion for now and get some sleep. Our shift will be here before we know it."

Jack waited for Dax to get off the bed, but Dax had already decided that the time had come for one of those little nudges he knew he would have to give Jack until he started to get comfortable and relax around him.

So instead he said, "You're right," and wiggled his way down in the bed and plopped his head on the pillow, all without letting go of Jack's hand.

"Oh," Jack said with a surprised look.

"You got a problem with me sleeping here?" Dax asked.

"I guess not," Jack said as he slid down on the bed to align his head with Dax's.

Dax reached over and placed a soft, gentle kiss on Jack's lips. "Good night, Jack."

Shocked and almost speechless yet again, Jack mumbled, "Good night, Dax."

JACK opened his eyes as the sun was slowly starting to peek through the little porthole above his bunk. He glanced at the clock just as the red LED number changed from five forty-one to five forty-two, and thought how oddly content he felt and didn't want to move. *Wow, I must have really been tired, I fell asleep fully clothed.* It took him just a second to remember the events of the previous night and see the arm holding him at the waist. *Oh, Jack, what have you done?* He immediately realized it was Dax's warm, lean body holding him snugly and providing that contentment he was experiencing. Dax's breathing was slow and steady, and he was purring like a kitten, so Jack knew he was still asleep. He fought the urge to bolt and tried to work his way through the panic.

This is okay, I'm okay. I'm still dressed, nothing happened. He calmed himself down, steadied his breathing, and lay still while he figured out what to do next. As he relaxed into the embrace of the man lying behind him, he realized it didn't feel as odd as he thought it would. Then he got a little miffed at himself. *What did it matter if something had happened? I'm a grown man, and if I want to sleep with another grown man, it's my business.* Dax started to move behind him, and he stiffened up, not knowing what to expect. Jack felt Dax bury his head in the crook of his neck and nibble on his neck lightly. A shiver ran up his spine, as the sensation felt strange but all too familiar somehow. He stretched his legs out completely, and Dax did the same. Through a stifled yawn, Dax whispered, "Hey."

"Hey," Jack said back.

"What time is it?"

Jack looked at the clock again and said, "Five forty-eight."

"Great, just enough time for a quick shower," Dax said. "Care to join me?"

Jack nervously laughed as Dax jumped out of bed like a man with a mission.

"Have you seen the showers on this boat?" Jack asked.

"Sure, why do you think I asked you?"

"Maybe another time," Jack said.

"I figured as much," Dax replied.

"Baby steps," Jack said. "Baby steps."

"Okay, see you when I see you," Dax said with a smile as he stooped down to pick up his shoes and then headed for the door. Midway he stopped, turned, took a leap, and landed right on top of Jack. "Do Dona and I need to pack our bags this morning or can we stay?" he asked.

Jack smiled. "I think we can give it another try, but we have to try and remember everything we said last night."

Dax kissed Jack on the lips and said, "Deal. Oh, and good morning, Jack." And just as quickly he was off of the bunk and out of the door.

Jack got up and sat on the edge of the bed and shook his head from side to side. *Why do I feel so cheap all of a sudden?*

He took a two-minute shower, slicked his blond hair back, and headed for the bridge.

"One minute to spare," Jack said with a big smile as he stepped onto the bridge. "Damn, I'm good."

Brad and Mac were in the captain's seats, watching the sun making its way above the horizon. "You're in a very chipper mood this morning, considering how you left here at two o'clock," Brad said.

"Oh really, I hadn't noticed," Jack responded.

"How was your *down time*?" Mac said as he used his fingers to make air quotes, never taking his eyes off of the horizon.

Jack used his fingers to make the same gesture when he said, "Oh, my *down time* was just fine, thank you."

"Come on, Jack, spill it."

"Spill what?" Jack asked with a slow, easy grin.

"Fine, keep it to yourself, but we'll find out," Mac said. "I don't think Dax is as tight-lipped as you are."

"Go for it," Jack said. "Dax is his own man and doesn't need me telling him what he can or cannot say."

Mac slid out of the seat and grabbed Brad's hand. "Let's go, Doc." Brad slid out of his seat as well and winked at Mac. "Let's stop by the crew berth on the way to our cabin, just to check in with Dona," he said. "And, Jack, I assume that since you and Dax made up, we're staying?"

"We're staying," Jack said as he started whistling. "And go right ahead, Dona will probably be in her cabin, but I'm sure Dax will be there too, and that's who you really want to talk to."

"We're counting on it," Mac said as they both walked off the bridge, hand in hand.

WHEN Mac and Brad got to the crew berth, Dax and Dona were just doing the handoff, discussing some sonar images Dona had printed during her shift. Dax had just told her that he'd fixed everything with Dax and they were continuing the expedition.

They both looked up to the smiling faces of Mac and Brad.

"Okay, Mr. Powers," Brad said. "Spill it."

Dona smiled and said, "Yeah, Dax, spill it. We got most of the business out of the way, now do tell."

Dax smiled. "Not much to tell, really. We talked for about an hour or so, then fell asleep."

"Together?" Brad asked.

"Yes, together, but we did nothing but sleep, and we were fully clothed."

"Are you kidding me?" Brad asked as he smiled at Dona.

"That's it," Dax said. "I told you there wasn't much to tell. I need to take this real slow with Jack. I don't want to push him away."

"Good idea," Mac said. "What's your plan?"

"Well, I don't really have one, but I think I'll start with playing it a little cool. I feel certain that he's the kind of guy that needs a challenge, so I'll be close, but not too close. Be sweet, but not too sweet. Be flirtatious, but not too flirtatious. It's important that he come to me if he truly wants this. I don't want to be seen as the aggressor who tried to coax him over to the wild side."

"Good point," Mac said, and turned to Brad with a weary look on his face. "Now, can we get some sleep?"

"Yep, let's go."

"Dona, are you coming?" Mac asked as they turned to leave.

"I'm right behind you," she said. "Just need a second to finish going over these sonar images with Dax before I turn in."

"Okay, see you in four hours," Brad said.

Dax and Dona reviewed the final images and decided a few of them were worth second looks, so they earmarked them for later that day. When they were finished, Dona folded up the charts and looked at Dax with a questioning look and took a deep breath.

"Do you know what you're doing?" she asked.

"Why, baby sister, I have no idea what you're talking about."

"We're twins, remember," she said. "Don't baby sister me."

"Yeah, but I was born first," Dax said with a smirk. "A full minute and a half before you, which makes me your older brother."

"Seriously, Dax, I hope you're not making a mistake. This expedition is too important to screw up over a straight man with bi-curious urges."

Dax looked down at the table and thought for a minute. "I really don't think it's a bi-curious thing. I think there could be something there, at least for me, and I hope for Jack too. You know me, Dona. When was the last time I just slept with someone, fully clothed, holding hands?"

"You've got me there, but just be careful, Dax. You really are playing with fire, and your heart and our expedition just might go up in flames."

"I guess I'm willing to take that chance, for something real," Dax said as he looked into Dona's eyes. "For the first time in a long time," he added.

As she stood, she reached over and squeezed his hand and smiled. "If you need me, you know where to find me," was the last thing she said as she stepped out of the little cabin.

She left Dax staring at the small computer screen, wondering what he'd just admitted to. *Jack and me*, he thought. *Is there really something there or am I just imagining it?*

He made up his mind in that second that he was going to find out. He wanted to call Jack and just ask him, but he didn't dare. He needed to play it cool. *For me to be sure, Jack has to come to me*, he thought. He'd give Jack a few minutes to get settled on the bridge before he radioed him with coordinates he wanted to revisit. He wouldn't mention anything about their night together.

Chapter 6

JACK was sitting at the helm, his attention split between the horizon and the autopilot. His mind wandered back to last night. The more he thought about it, the more comfortable he felt. *Maybe Brad and Mac were right, maybe I am gay, or at least bisexual. Let's face it. I've never had a successful relationship with a woman, ever. Could I have been so deep in the closet that even I didn't know I was gay? Maybe subconsciously I was just burying my attraction to guys because I didn't want to be gay. I've never really been around gay people, until Brad and now Mac, and they seem happy. People don't seem to care that they are together, not that they go screaming it from the rooftops. Oh my God, I've got to stop this, it's rapid-fire thinking, I'm gonna short-circuit. But Dax is an awfully hot guy, and I liked sleeping in his arms.*

Jack was startled from his thoughts by Dax's voice. "Base to bridge. Jack, are you there?"

Jack smiled and removed the handheld radio from the hook. He didn't want to seem too anxious, so he paused and took a deep breath before he pressed the button to speak.

"Bridge here, hey, Dax," he responded.

"Hey, Jack, do you have something handy to write with?"

"Uh, yeah," Jack said as he leaned over the helm and grabbed a pen and pad.

"I have some coordinates I'd like to revisit from last night. You ready?"

"Shoot."

"Okay, Latitude, 58.9748 north and longitude, 135.227 west," Dax said.

"Got it. You want to change course now?"

"Can we?"

"Sure, give me a couple minutes to plug these numbers into the GPS and we'll be ready to go," Jack responded. "I'll radio you when we reach our destination."

"Roger that," Dax said. "Thanks, Jack, base out."

Wow, that was short, Jack thought as put the radio back on the hook. Not a "How are you?" "It was great sleeping with you." "I enjoyed last night." Nothing. Men...!

When Jack reached the location, he radioed Dax. "Bridge to Base, Dax do you read?"

"Loud and clear," Dax responded.

"We're here. What would you like me to do?"

"How long can you hold the position without dropping the hook?"

"We have a steady wind coming out of the north at about twelve knots, and the current is running about five knots. If I can keep the bow into the wind and get the speed adjusted, maybe ten minutes or so," he said.

"That's all the time I need, thanks, Jack."

"Base out."

The way the grid system worked, the wreck could be just three hundred yards to port, but it might take them a day and a half to get to that point on the grid as they worked their way along the imaginary lines. Once Dax was sure they hadn't missed anything, he radioed Jack to pick up his previous position and continue to the next waypoint on the grid.

Jack spent the next five minutes adjusting his forward speed to match the current and attempting to hold his location utilizing his bow and stern thrusters.

Down in the little crew berth, Dax studied the computer screen, leaning in to get a closer look and then backing away for a bigger view. He printed each image and would later put them together to form a larger picture of his target area. He didn't see anything out of the ordinary this time, but Dona thought she'd noticed something the first go-round. He knew very well that sometimes things you missed in a single image, developed into a shape or object when you saw the images pieced together. He would pass these images on to Dona for a fresh set of eyes, to make sure he didn't miss anything, but his gut told him he was very close.

The next few weeks went very smoothly. Everyone fell into a comfortable rhythm, changing shifts, reviewing sonar images, preparing meals, and maintaining the boat. Dax had wanted to drag Jack down to his cabin and have his way with him several times a day, but he did his best to restrain himself. They seemed to be getting to know one another at a good pace, and Dax thought that Jack was getting more and more comfortable with their semi-relationship. Occasionally they would fall asleep on the couch, but nothing was happening but a little light kissing and a lot of snuggling. Dax made sure Jack knew he was interested, but he let Jack take the lead, and he didn't push. For Dax, that was the hardest thing. He always went after what he wanted; it was just his personality. But not this time. He thought Jack was worth the wait, and hoped he would come around sooner rather than later.

Jack, on the other hand, was getting very frustrated with Dax's flirtatious behavior. He spent his shifts and time off consumed with thoughts of the handsome treasure hunter and what had transpired between them in the last few weeks. He thought he wanted to explore something with Dax, but he didn't want to be gay. But how could he be attracted to Dax and *not* be gay? Could he have it both ways? He thought not. But in the end, it probably didn't matter anyway, because all they ever really did was make out and snuggle, and that was starting to send a strong message. Maybe Dax was just teasing him and was not really interested.

He found himself relieved and pissed all at the same time. For the first time in his lonely little life, he was sexually frustrated, and over a man, which confused him more than ever. He didn't know how to make the first move, so he decided he would talk to Mac and Brad and get their take on it when his shift was over and they came to relieve him. But before he could get another thought through his tangled mind, he heard that familiar voice he was getting so used to—and if he was honest with himself, looked forward to hearing.

"Base to bridge," Dax said.

Jack picked up the radio and said, "Bridge here. Hey, Dax what's up?"

"Can you hold our position? I see something very interesting, but I need to get a better look at the sonar reading."

"I'll try, but the winds have kicked up in the last hour," Jack responded.

"Just do your best, and hold her as long as you can," Dax said in a reassuring tone.

"Roger that," Jack said.

Dax stared at the sonar image and blinked his eyes several times. He was seeing a drastic change in the topography of the underwater landscape, which was usually a clue that he was looking at some sort of obstruction. The obstruction was long enough to be a ship, but it was oddly shaped. Dax knew that the shape could be the result of years of sea growth and sediment deforming the look of the vessel.

"Jack!" Dax called.

"Bridge," Jack responded.

"Can you move ten degrees to port? I think I see something, but it's on the edge of the sonar reading." Jack couldn't help but notice the excitement in Dax's voice. He sounded like a little boy at Christmas, and the thought of Dax in his little footy pajamas on Christmas morning made him smile.

"Yep, give me a minute." Jack hit the port thrusters, and the *Lindsey C* began to slowly move to starboard, inch by inch.

"Perfect, stop!" Dax shouted. "What's our depth?"

Jack glanced at the depth finder as he released the thrusters, and the boat slowly stopped its sideward motion.

"Thirty-three and a half feet," he shouted into the radio.

"Great! Drop the hook," Dax shrieked. "We're going to launch the ROV to get a better look."

"Got it," Jack responded.

Jack hit his anchor release button and did his best again to stabilize the vessel as the anchor slowly descended into the cold, blue-gray waters of the Lynn Canal.

With the anchor set, Jack was shutting down the engines when the door to the bridge flew open, and he saw Dax grinning from ear to ear. Dax closed the door behind him and walked across the bridge and stopped right in front of Jack. Jack looked into Dax's gleaming, hazel eyes and held his gaze. They stood toe to toe, eyes locked in a sensual stare.

"My gut tells me we have something," Dax said, his eyes never looking away from Jack's.

"Really?" Jack whispered.

"Yeah," Dax responded in a sultry voice. "But I need to launch *Hunter II* to get a better look. If we see what I think we'll see, we'll make the first dive of the expedition."

"*Hunter II?*" Jack asked.

Dax lifted his arms and put them on Jack's shoulders. "Yeah, the ROV."

Never breaking eye contact, he leaned in and gently kissed Jack on the lips. When Jack didn't pull away, Dax went in for a deeper kiss. Jack hesitantly leaned into the kiss, and Dax ran one of his hands through Jack's shoulder-length blond hair and rested it on the back of his neck. Dax pressed his tongue against Jack's closed lips, seeking entry, and Jack willingly opened to the request. Jack closed his eyes and went with the moment as their tongues softly tangoed to the rhythm of their hearts beating. Dax moved his other hand from Jack's shoulder and softly stroked his muscled back as he further explored the inside of Jack's warm and inviting mouth. Jack, not wanting Dax to move, finally raised his arms to Dax's waist and slipped them behind his back and held him close. Jack was really getting into the moment when the bridge door flew open yet again, and Mac and Brad stepped onto the bridge. Visibly shaken, Jack broke the kiss, let his hands fall to his side, and stepped away from Dax.

"Oops," Brad said, smiling warmly. "Don't let us stop you."

"Stop what?" Jack said nervously. "Dax was just telling me that we need to launch the ROV and do a reconnaissance dive."

"Boy, that was some conversation," Mac said.

"Very funny," Jack shot back.

Dax, up to this point, had stood motionless and had been very silent. He smiled as Brad and Mac eyed him closely then eyed Jack in the same manner.

"Tell them what you found, Dax," Jack said to try and change the subject.

"Give me a minute to get Dona up here so everyone can hear at the same time."

He radioed for Dona, and when she reached the bridge, he filled them all in on what he'd found. Everyone was given a job, and they all went in their own directions. Suddenly it was Dax and Jack on the bridge, alone again. Jack looked at Dax and blushed as he looked down at his instruments—anywhere but at Dax.

"I'm over here," Dax said.

"I know where you are," Jack said.

"Then look at me."

Dax took Jack's hands in his and looked into those gorgeous, blue eyes.

"Do you want me, Jack?" Dax asked.

"No... yes... I don't know," Jack responded as he slipped his hands out of Dax's and turned away.

Dax looked crushed, but he smiled and whispered, "Okay, Jack, I'll back off."

He turned and took a step toward the door. Jack panicked and grabbed him by the arm to stop him. Dax stopped momentarily and waited. Jack tried to speak, but nothing came out. He cleared his throat and tried again.

"Dax, please," was all he could say.

Dax looked back and met Jack's pleading stare. "I've let you know on more than one occasion that I'm interested. Now the ball's in your court," he said as he left the bridge.

Jack collapsed into his captain's seat and put his head in his hands. He rubbed his face and eyes and laid his head back and thought, *What in the hell is happening to me?*

DONA, Brad, and Mac were preparing the *Hunter II* when Dax made his way up on deck.

"Everything okay?" Mac asked as he continued to prepare the submersible.

"Fine as frog's hair," Dax said sarcastically.

"I mean between you and Jack," Mac continued.

"I know what you mean," Dax said. "I don't know, he's really confused and doesn't know what he wants. I won't push. He's got to make the next move."

"I'll talk to him," Mac said as he laid his hand on Dax's shoulder.

"I appreciate that, Mac, but don't press him. This is not just about sex or a relationship with another guy, it's about his entire life. Can you imagine believing all of your life that you were one thing and then suddenly realizing that you were something else?" Dax asked.

"Actually, I can," Mac said. "I was very happily married to Jack's sister Lindsey when she was diagnosed with breast cancer."

Dona stopped what she was doing and looked up with a puzzled expression on her face.

"When she died, I focused all my attention on our daughter Zoe-Grace, but when Zoe went away to college, I realized just how truly alone and lost I really was. For the next few years, I simply went through the motions of living, until Brad walked back into my life. I'd met Brad and his partner Jeff years before, when I would fly them up to Hiline Lake for vacation a couple times a year. After Jeff died of cancer, Brad was trying to escape and came up to the lake, and we reconnected. It started out with me helping Brad through something I had already been through, and over a year's time, it turned into something way more than friendship. I struggled a little at first, but realized that life was too short for labels. Lindsey would always say, 'Love has no boundaries,' and boy was she ever right."

Mac looked at Brad and said, "And... I've never looked back."

Dona and Dax looked at each other, and you could have heard a pin drop.

"Wow," Dona said. "I had no idea. What a story."

"Isn't it?" Brad said. "And the funniest part of the story, which Mac conveniently left out, was that Jack was furious with us. He couldn't believe how Mac could be straight one minute and gay the next. It took him quite a while to get used to the idea, but he eventually came around."

Dax smiled. "Really?" he asked.

"Yep, but we always thought Jack might be gay, he was *so* homophobic back then," Brad said.

Dona slapped the side of the *Hunter II* and said, "I think he's good to go."

Just then Jack walked out on deck, looking a little weary.

"Would you like to use the dinghy winch to lower the *Hunter II* over the side?" he asked.

"That's a great idea," Dona replied.

Brad and Mac carried the submersible to the bow of the boat. Jack unhooked the dinghy from the winch cable and secured it to the ROV. The winch lifted the *Hunter II* off of the deck and the large arm swung it out over the side. Dona held on to the cable that would secure it to the boat until it made its descent. As the ROV hung out over the side of the boat, Dax went down to home base and flipped on three computer monitors, one for each camera, to make sure all the equipment was working properly. He moved the controls for the arms and then the controls for the cameras. His hand froze when he saw Jack on one of the monitors. The lens was positioned fully on Jack as he stood with his back to the camera. This was the first time he could really study Jack without Jack's knowledge, and he liked what he saw. The man's broad shoulders formed a perfect v-shape down to his small waist and well-rounded butt. He was built—not over-built but truly gorgeous. It was more than his looks, though; it was the way in which he carried himself. Just standing there, not really moving, he commanded attention. Dax's dick started to fill, and he actually felt himself blushing. He focused the other two cameras on Jack and continued watching the man on three computer monitors as he chatted with Mac. Dax was getting harder with every second, and his dick was begging to be released from the confines of his tight blue jeans. He kept taking peeks at the door as if he thought someone might come in, but other than that, he never took his eyes off of Jack.

I am so going to hate myself if I do this, Dax thought as he unbuttoned his jeans, slid the metal zipper down, reached inside his boxer briefs, and took his dick in his hand. He stared at the computer screen, unblinking, as he rubbed his hand over his cock. He had never done anything like this in front of a computer screen, and it really felt weird, like a voyeur, but he couldn't stop himself. Droplets of pearly white precum were leaking from the head of his dick, and Dax used his thumb to smear it around his blood-filled bulb. "You're a gorgeous son of a bitch, you know that?" he whispered to the computer screen, as if he were talking directly to Jack. He started to stroke his dick slowly at first, then something overtook him, and he suddenly felt a strong sense of urgency that he'd never experienced with sex before. He moved his hand feverishly over his dick, licking his lips at the size of Jack's broad shoulders and perfectly rounded ass. Eyes still on his video lover, Dax continued to stroke his rock-hard dick, and he was getting very close.

Then suddenly, as if Jack knew exactly what Dax was doing, he looked directly at the camera and shyly licked his lips. That very move sent Dax over the edge, and he came harder than he could ever remember. He milked his dick until every last drop was expelled, never taking his eyes off of the man that made his knees weak.

Dax heard Dona's voice come over the radio.

"Dax, what are you doing down there? Is all the equipment working properly?"

Dax, with his dick still hanging out and his jeans soiled with cum, picked up the radio and said, "Roger that, everything is in perfect working condition." He smiled as he looked down at his dick. Good working condition, all right. "I'll be right up for the launch," he chuckled.

"What's so funny?" Dona asked.

"Oh, nothing, I'll be up after a quick stop in the head."

Dax quickly zipped up his jeans and ran to his cabin. He took his soiled jeans and underwear off and quickly slipped on a clean pair of jeans, not bothering to put on underwear, and quickly joined the rest of the crew topside.

Dax could see Jack watching him oddly as he strolled across the deck toward Dona, and he felt himself blushing again. When their eyes met, Jack's lips broke into a demure smile, and Dax sensed that somehow Jack knew exactly what he'd been doing down below.

Dax broke the eye contact between him and Jack and turned his attention to Dona and the ROV. "Let's get this baby in the water," he said.

WITH Jack now at the winch controls on the bridge, Dona guided him via the radio as he slowly lowered the submersible into the water, while she fed the cabling that tethered the vessel to the boat. As the *Hunter II* floated lazily on the surface, Dax again went down below to make sure they were getting a good feed from the cameras and could begin the submersible's descent. Dona detached the tether, and the little submersible started its wireless descent. When the others could no longer see the ROV, they joined Dax below deck.

"The underwater visibility is great today," Dax said as he guided the ROV to the proper coordinates using the handheld control panel. Everyone was excited and focusing their attention on the computer screens, including Jack. He was standing right behind Dax's chair and, without realizing it, he rested both hands on Dax's shoulders. Surprised, Dax looked up at him and smiled. When Jack realized what he'd done, he fought the urge to quickly yank his hands back, not wanting to offend Dax; he allowed his hands to rest there until he could think of a reason to casually remove them.

Forgetting about the computer screen in front of him, Jack stared at his hands resting on Dax's shoulders. Suddenly, he felt like he was free-falling. How could a simple touch make a person feel so lightheaded and strange? He felt like there was an energy being passed through him and Dax, and he wondered if Dax felt it as well. He didn't have to wonder long, because within seconds, controlling the ROV with his right hand, Dax raised his left hand across his chest, rested it on top of Jack's, and squeezed. The two men stayed that way while the *Hunter II* continued its descent. With Jack's hands on him, Dax found it very hard to concentrate on the task at hand, but he knew he had to snap out of it and get the job done or Dona would give him a great deal of grief.

Noticing movement out of the corner of his eye, Brad turned his head in Jack's direction. What he saw put a huge smile on his face. He elbowed Mac. "What?" Mac whispered, but didn't break eye contact with the computer screen. Brad elbowed him again. Seemingly annoyed with the interruption, Mac turned to see what was so important. Their eyes met and Brad nodded in Jack's direction. When Mac saw what was happening, a huge grin spread across his face as well. He looked back at Brad, and they both turned their attention back to Jack.

Jack must have sensed them staring and slowly turned his head. He looked at Mac, then at Brad, and instantly felt the blush consume his entire face. He again had to fight the urge to withdraw his hands and break contact with Dax's body. Jack stood there, frozen in time, and then it hit him like a ton of bricks. *The more power I give them, the more they are going to torture me. I'll never live this down, so why not go for it. They're not going to intimidate me.* He felt the initial blush and embarrassment start to subside, and then he was just plain pissed.

I'll dare them. If they want a show, by God, that's what they'll get. It wasn't that long ago that they were in the same situation. Let the show begin.

Jack defiantly glared at Brad and Mac. He started to softly massage Dax's shoulders and neck. At the sudden sensation, Dax looked up in surprise. When he did, Jack leaned over and placed a long, wet kiss right on Dax's lips. Stunned, Dax leaned into the kiss. When Jack was through kissing Dax, he looked over at Brad and Mac and smirked. He kissed the top of Dax's head, never breaking eye contact with Brad and Mac. "Anything else I can do for you, boys?" he asked.

Dona was concentrating on the computer images and seemed to be oblivious to the entire episode. She looked up, a confused expression on her face. "What did I miss?"

Jack angrily stared at Brad and Mac and said, "What did she miss, gentlemen?"

Mac and Brad looked at each other. "Oh nothing," Mac said. "We're just having a little fun."

"At my expense," Jack added.

He turned his attention back to Dax and continued to massage his neck as he watched the computer screen.

Dax guided the ROV toward its destination, and tried to remember everything he'd read about the *Anna Wyoming*. He pictured every image over and over in his mind and started whispering to himself. "One-hundred-and-fifty-one feet in length, built in 1871 at a Camden, New Jersey shipyard on the Delaware River. Very innovative for her time, she was one of the first vessels constructed from iron. She had two modes of propulsion, a three-masted schooner sailing rig, and a state-of-the-art steeple compound engine. She had a draft of nine feet and could sustain a speed of eight knots." Dax knew that remembering the ship's physical attributes could possibly help him identify a portion of the ship if it had broken into pieces during its demise, or simply rested intact on her port or starboard sides. If the mast and stack were still intact, it would be very easy to identify her just by knowing what to look for.

Dax checked the submersible's course, depth, and location and knew it was nearing the chartered coordinates. He released Jack's hand and placed both hands on the control panel.

After squeezing both shoulders twice, as if to signal the end of the massage, Jack removed his hands from Dax's shoulders and stepped back. Jack was surprised at the overwhelming need to touch Dax again, but he resisted the urge and held his ground. He knew Dax would need to concentrate and use both hands to maneuver the submersible in and around the area, in addition to using all three cameras and the two extension arms.

Observing Dax in his element gave Jack a whole new perspective of the man he was getting to know. He worked the controls of the submersible like he was the great and powerful Wizard of Oz. His touch was very subtle, and the *Hunter II* responded like a loyal golden retriever. As the ROV fought the swift currents and dove deeper toward the bottom, Dax switched on the bright headlights, and within minutes, the ocean floor came into view. Dax and the ROV investigated every mound of coral, every hill of silt, and anything that even resembled a protrusion from the canal floor. During the next few hours, Dona studied charts and kept Dax company while the others came and went as activities demanded. Occasionally Dona would take over for Dax while he stretched his legs and took a bathroom break, but they had done this drill many times before and were very comfortable alternating positions. With only an hour of daylight left, Brad and Mac went to the galley to start preparing dinner, and Jack went up to the bridge to check on equipment and check the weather forecast for that night and the next day. Dax was just about to give up for the day when he saw what he thought could be a propeller shaft jutting out from a large mound on the canal floor.

"Well I'll be damned," Dax muttered as he stared at the computer screen. Dona looked up from her charts with a quizzical look on her face. Dax moved the ROV up and back to get a better look at the big picture.

Dax pointed his index finger to an object on the screen and said, "Dona, what does that look like to you?"

"I'd bet my life that's a propeller shaft," she said with a grin.

"I'd bet your life too," he responded.

"Very funny," she said with a smirk. "Can we get a better look?"

Dax adjusted the joystick and the ROV slowly moved to starboard and backed away for a different angle. The way the shaft seemed to disappear into the large mound only confirmed their suspicions.

Dax reached for the radio and said, "Base to bridge, Jack, come back."

"Bridge here," Jack said.

"Hey, Jack, I think we've found something. Get Brad and Mac, and get down here."

Jack found Brad and Mac in the galley and they quickly made their way down to the cabin. They gathered around the computer screen as Dax pointed out what he and Dona hoped was the propeller shaft of the *Anna Wyoming*. From his research, Dax knew that the ship had an iron hull, and although it would rust and disintegrate over time, the outline of the hull should still be somewhat visible. Dax tried to bring the ROV up to get a wider view, but unfortunately, with the daylight fading, the lights were not strong enough to penetrate to the bottom, and they simply stared into darkness.

"Well, that settles it," Dax said shutting off the computer monitor and looking up at Dona. "Reconnaissance dive at first light?" she asked.

Dax nodded his head. "Let's get the *Hunter II* up and secured for the night, and then let's eat," he said. "I'm starved."

"I think that's our cue," Mac said to Brad. "Do you need us on deck?"

"I think Jack and I can manage," Dax said as he winked at Jack.

"You boys handle the *Hunter II*, and I'll get everything down here secured for the night," Dona added.

While Dona worked down below, Dax grabbed the radio and the remote control for the ROV and headed to the deck, as Jack made his way to the bridge. When Dax reached the deck, he surfaced the ROV and maneuvered it to the swim platform so he could hook up the tether. He walked the ROV alongside the hull to the bow and connected the cable to the winch. He radioed Jack that the ROV was connected and ready to be lifted safely onto the deck. Jack joined Dax topside, and together they secured the *Hunter II* to its riggings for the night.

When everything was secured, the sun was just starting to dip below the horizon, and Jack stopped to watch. Dax joined him and put his arm gently on his shoulder, and together they watched the spectacular swirls of pinks, oranges, and reds all blended together to form a perfect sunset. Jack, unable to control himself, turned to Dax and gently kissed him on the cheek.

"What was that for?" Dax asked.

"Oh, nothing. I just felt like doing it," Jack said.

"Wanna do it again?" Dax asked with a smile.

"Maybe," Jack said.

Dax's smile faded, and he started to ramble. "Well, Captain Cameron, don't do me any fav—"

Jack put his lips over Dax's mid-ramble and smothered him with a long, savory kiss. Jack's tongue fought for entry, and when Dax's lips parted, he found solace in the warmth of Dax's mouth. Their tongues roamed and searched each other's welcoming mouths until they were both out of breath.

When Jack pulled away and left Dax's swollen lips bare, they were both panting.

"Eureka," Jack said. "Now I know what to do to shut you up," he teased.

"If all I need to do is go on a tirade to get you to kiss me, look out, Jack. Your life is about to become very confrontational."

"Okay, maybe I'll rethink that statement and save us both the trouble and just kiss you more."

"I think that's a great idea," Dax said.

Just as Jack was leaning in to kiss Dax a second time, Brad popped up on deck.

"Dinner's ready, you two."

"As usual, your timing is impeccable," Jack said.

"Oh, did I interrupt something?" he asked.

"Nothing that can't be continued later," Dax said as he winked at Jack.

Brad spun on his heels with Jack and Dax in tow, and they made their way to the little galley. Dinner was a pork roast Mac had put in the slow cooker that morning, accompanied by mashed potatoes, mixed vegetables, and warm French bread. They ate with a renewed excitement after the day's discovery and discussed plans for the next morning. Dax, Dona, and Jack would do tomorrow's dive, with Brad and Mac staying aboard to man the ship. If their assumptions were true, and this was the wreck of the *Anna Wyoming*, they would have to leave the site and immediately report their find, in person, to the proper authorities and stake their claim to the salvage rights. They would then head right back to the site to start the salvage operation. When dinner was through and the galley was cleaned, it was nearing eleven o'clock. Brad and Mac turned in, with Dona right behind them.

Jack looked at Dax in nervous anticipation. "Um, I'm gonna check on the bridge before I turn in. Want to take a walk with me?"

"Sure," Dax said. "I'll check on the *Hunter II* and make sure everything is secure, and I'll meet you on the bow."

"Perfect," Jack said, and the two men made their way topside. Jack secured the bridge for the night and strolled to the bow. He stood at the bowsprit and stared out into the darkness. Dax finished checking the ROV and walked over to join Jack.

Dax walked up behind Jack and slid his arms around Jack's waist. Deep in thought, Jack jumped at the touch, but relaxed immediately.

"Everything okay?" Dax whispered.

"How did you know?" Jack said in a hushed voice.

"Know what?" Dax asked.

"That you liked guys."

Dax thought before he answered, knowing that his answer held a great deal of significance to Jack. "I guess I always knew," he said. "But I didn't know what it meant until I was a teenager."

"That's right," Jack remembered. "You were homeschooled."

Dax nodded. "Jack, have you never thought about another guy in a sexual way before?"

Jack thought hard but said, "I can't say that I have."

After a long silence, Dax asked, "So what makes you think you're gay?"

"I think you're hot as hell, and I love kissing you and, well... you're a guy."

"Good answer, and thanks for noticing," Dax chuckled. "I feel the same way."

"You do?" Jack asked.

"Jack, how could you not know that?" Dax asked. "But look," he added. "If you decide that this is something you want to explore, I will do my best to take the journey with you, but you have to take the lead. This has to be your decision and yours alone."

"I know all that," Jack said. "Why do you think I've been so apprehensive?"

"And you have to really be sure if and when anything happens between us. I'm not a science experiment. You can't sleep with me then throw me away if you decide you're not gay. Are we clear?"

Jack thought about what Dax was saying. "We're clear," he said.

"So, we're on the same page?" Dax asked.

"I think so."

"Now shut up and kiss me," Dax pleaded.

With Dax's arms still holding him loosely around the waist, Jack slowly turned and put his arms around Dax's neck. "My pleasure," he said with a grin.

They necked like high-school sweethearts for a little while longer until Dax finally admitted, "We have an early morning. What do you say we turn in?"

Jack raised one eyebrow and looked at Dax, questioning.

"To separate cabins, you idiot," Dax said.

Jack smiled and held out his elbow. "Please allow me, sir."

Dax slipped his arm into Jack's and said, "Chivalry is not dead after all."

"Not while I'm still breathing," Jack said as he escorted Dax to his cabin.

They were so into their little game that neither of them felt the stare of distant night vision binoculars, or heard the almost-silent click of a camera documenting their every move.

WHEN they got to Dax's cabin door, Dax slid his arm out of Jack's and they stood, nervously wondering what should happen next. In the past, Dax had never been shy about going after what he wanted, but this time he didn't want to make the first move. Being several inches taller than Jack, he looked down and saw the most beautiful crystal-blue eyes gazing up adoringly and locked on his. Dax could almost see a battle raging behind them. Both lust and confusion clouded Jack's baby blues, and it tugged at Dax's heartstrings. If Dax pushed, he felt certain that he could convince Jack to spend the night with him, but at what cost? If it didn't go well, it could affect the rest of their lives—for different reasons, of course. So he did nothing. It was at that very moment that Dax realized he was falling in love with Captain Jackson P. Cameron, and that particular thought sent shivers of fear mixed with excitement down his spine.

AS JACK looked up into the dreamiest hazel eyes he'd ever seen, he realized just how much he wanted Dax. But something, or someone, held him back. He knew that once he stepped into Dax's cabin, there was no turning back. Could he do this? He wasn't sure. Yes, he wanted Dax—hell, he even needed him—but was it lust, or was it more? He couldn't use Dax as an experiment. He had to be sure. *Not yet*, he thought. *Not until I'm sure.*

Instead of opening the cabin door, he rose up on his toes and placed his lips against Dax's. The waiting lips were warm and supple and opened for him without delay. Jack's tongue teased at the taut flesh of Dax's warm, sweet mouth. His hands moved to grab Dax's dark head, feeling the silky hair slide between his fingers as his tongue slid between his lips. The heat was building, and Jack knew if he didn't stop soon, he wouldn't, so he withdrew and once again gazed into Dax's sultry eyes. He moved his mouth to Dax's ear and whispered, "Good night, Dax."

Dax responded in kind, then slowly opened the door and retreated to his cabin. When he closed the cabin door, Jack placed his palms against the door, as if trying not to break the connection, but it was too late. He fought the urge to slam his palms against the door until Dax opened it and allowed him to enter, but instead he lowered his head in frustration. He took a deep breath and then stepped away from the door and retreated to his empty cabin.

Dax sensed that Jack was still standing outside his door and imagined his palms coming up and resting against it. He slowly placed his hands where he imagined the other man's to be and held them there until he heard Jack's footsteps fade into the salon.

Chapter 7

DAYBREAK came very early, and everyone started the day with anticipation of what was to come. Brad and Mac were up first and had breakfast going when, one by one, the rest of the crew joined them in the galley. Throughout the idle chatter of their normal breakfast conversation, they went over last-minute details about their day. Immediately after breakfast, Brad and Mac left the galley to prepare the dive equipment while the others stayed behind to clean and discuss the underwater conditions and strategy for the dive.

"Once under the surface," Dax explained, "we'll start our dive at what we hope is a propeller shaft and go from there. According to Jack's reading yesterday, the deepest part of the dive would be no more than thirty-five feet, and as you know, that eliminates or greatly reduces the risk of decompression sickness, nitrogen narcosis, or oxygen toxicity."

They all nodded in agreement.

"Normally," Dax continued, "the shallow depth would allow us to remain under the surface for a much longer period of time, but because the water temperature is hovering between thirty-nine and forty-one degrees we will be very susceptible to hypothermia and will need to closely monitor our body temperature gauges and limit our dive to about forty-five minutes."

"I know your first objective is to identify the wreck, but if you do that, what are the other objectives for this dive?" Jack asked.

"You're right, Jack," Dax said. "The first dive will be to determine if this is indeed the *Anna Wyoming*. If we're successful in that task, then we'll try to determine what condition the hull is in. In turn, that will dictate how we proceed."

"Forgive my ignorance," Jack said, "but how so?"

"Well," Dax shared, "if the hull is breached, once we have our salvage rights, we'll start by laying down a baseline grid and then do multiple dives to document the site with video, still digital cameras, and basic sketch-mapping techniques before we start the excavation. If the hull is intact, we know that everything on board is contained within its walls, and in that case, we'll use low-impact underwater explosives to open the ship's hull for entry and salvage."

"Got it," Jack said.

"Now, once inside the hull," Dax explained, "we go directly in search of the cargo hold. According to the documentation we found, the valuable mystery cargo was being kept in the cargo hold in the center hull of the ship."

"Is that typical?" Jack asked.

"Not really," Dona said. "But if the amount of gold rumored to be on board is accurate, the purser's safe would not be able to contain such a large sum, so the cargo hold would be the next logical spot."

Dax took over again. "However, also according to our records, the purser's safe is holding some valuable contents, and we certainly won't leave it if we can help it."

"Months of research," Dona added, "has given Dax a very detailed layout of the ship, and we know approximately where the cargo hold should be and therefore where we should start the search."

"Any other questions?" Dax asked.

"Nope," Jack said. "I'm good."

"Then let's get this show on the road," Dona exclaimed.

WITH a game plan and lots of excitement, they headed topside to suit up. When they reached the deck, their equipment was ready and waiting for them. Like good divers always do, they checked and rechecked Brad and Mac's work, making sure their buoyancy vests— better known as BC's—and regulators were attached properly and everything was in perfect working condition. The special dry suits designed to help keep them warm were difficult to get into and required a great deal of effort and time, so an hour quickly passed before they were ready for their descent. They made their way to the swim platform and put on their fins. Brad handed each one their full face masks, which included digital ultrasonic transceivers allowing them to communicate with the boat and each other under the surface with excellent voice clarity. Brad and Mac each carried a handheld radio receiver so they could communicate with the underwater team at all times. The three divers stood on the swim platform and, one by one, jumped into the cold Alaskan waters. When each had given the diver's universal "okay" sign by touching the top of their heads, they deflated their BC's and started their descent.

Dax had made hundreds of dives in his career, but each time he dropped below the surface of the water he was amazed by the sensation he felt and the things he saw. Today was no different; the aqua-colored water was clear as a bell and visibility was at least twenty to thirty feet. It appeared that the area surrounding the wreck was partially protected by a reef complex that provided a limited shield from the strong currents, but also provided an array of colorful fish and other sea life that made the reef their home. They swam along for the next twenty-five minutes in the shallow depths of fifteen to thirty feet, depending on the stage of the tide, and after swimming the length of the area several times, Dax finally said, "Well, guys, I feel certain we have a wreck here."

"I agree," Dona said. "But is it the *Anna Wyoming*?"

"Too soon to tell," Dax responded. "I don't see any visible evidence yet, but some of the characteristics of the site point in that direction."

"Like what?" Jack asked.

"For starters, the bow and stern are pretty badly beaten up, and based on the weather conditions on the night she went down, she would have taken a major beating along the reef system, so that supports our theory. In addition, what we assumed was a propeller shaft from the surface is indeed just that, and is about the length and size of the shaft that would have been on the steeple compound engine aboard the *Anna Wyoming*."

Dona gestured to another section of the site and added. "We know that the *Anna Wyoming* had a double-bottom iron hull, and there appears to be parts of that hull exposed over there. And those mounds to the left appear to be pieces of machinery attached to the base of one of the remaining steel masts. And lastly, her bow is pointing toward the north, and pieces of her iron plates are sticking out of that offending rock that juts nearly to the surface."

Dax took over again. "All these findings, combined with the fact that, when you look down from above, you can get a clear outline of the ship's orientation—and her length appears to be approximately the same length of the *Anna Wyoming*—gives us a pretty good idea that we are right on track. Whatever this ship's history, it's pretty obvious that she went down in very similar conditions and circumstances as the *Anna Wyoming*. And lastly, I can't see any signs that the interior hull is breached."

"Is that good or bad?" Jack asked.

"Sometimes it works in our favor, and sometimes it works against us," Dax said. "It's just too soon to tell."

"Wow, I'm really impressed," was all Jack could say. "You guys know your stuff."

"Thanks," they responded simultaneously.

"Now can we get out of this freezing water?" Dax asked.

"I'm with you," Jack answered.

"Lightweights," Dona mumbled as she rolled her eyes and started to swim in the direction of the boat. Dax and Jack exchanged a quick smile, then followed closely behind her as they began their ascent.

When they reached the surface, Brad and Mac were on deck and quickly made their way down to the swim platform. Mac helped each of them climb on to the boat as Brad helped them off with their gear. The boys had been listening in on the underwater conversation and didn't try to hide their anticipation. Dax and Dona gave them the *Reader's Digest* version again and told them they would fill them in with more details over lunch.

THEY feasted on turkey club sandwiches and chips while they excitedly discussed the morning's findings. They would make their second dive later that afternoon, but in the meantime, Dax wanted to review his notes and study the photos of the *Anna Wyoming* one more time, in hopes of finding some sort of markings that would help them identify the wreck and give them the proof they needed to stake their claim. If he couldn't find any visible markings, he would have no choice but to use underwater explosives to remove some of the one hundred years of growth surrounding the wreck in order to breach the hull.

After lunch, Dax and Dona spread all their research and photos on the galley table and started going over everything very closely. Jack, in full captain's mode, knew that in their current position, the weather could change drastically from hour to hour, so he headed to the fly bridge to check the latest weather reports, with Brad and Mac in tow. When they reached the bridge, Jack flipped his VHF radio to the weather frequency and sat in his captain's seat. Brad hopped into the seat next to him with his legs spread, and Mac scooted in between Brad's legs, facing forward and leaning his butt on the front of the seat. They listened in silence while the radio squawked its continuously looped prerecorded updates. When the radio reached the end of the loop and started over, Jack reached over and switched the radio back to channel sixteen. Brad finally broke the silence. "Sooooo, Jack, anything you want to talk to us about?"

"Nope, not that I can think of," Jack said in a teasing tone. "Other than the weather, and it looks pretty good for the afternoon dive, but I guess you heard that for yourself."

"Oh yeah, the weather, perfect, beautiful, got it. What about your little rendezvous last night?" Brad asked.

"Are you birds spying on me now?" Jack asked.

"Not really," Mac said. "We went up on deck for sunset last night and were quite amused to see Dax in your arms and your tongue down his throat."

Jack took a deep breath and let it out. "Okay, guys, I give. Go ahead and let me have it. I know I have it coming."

"Do you mean you *have it coming* because of all the grief you gave us when you found out that Mac and I were in love?" Brad asked.

"Yeah, among other things," Jack said. "Maybe I had a problem with your relationship because I was struggling with something myself."

"Ya think?" Mac said.

"Come on, guys, give me a break here."

"Did you give us one?" Mac asked, starting to get agitated. "I almost lost my life *and* Brad because of you and your stupid homophobia."

Brad placed his hands on Mac's shoulders and squeezed.

Jack looked down at the floor. "I know," he said in a whisper. "I'm really sorry."

"Okay, Mac, I think we've tortured him enough," Brad said. "I think he's learned his lesson on how not to be a bigot."

"Thanks a lot, Brad," Jack said. "But you guys have gotta help me here. I don't know what to do. I'm really attracted to Dax, and I think he likes me too, but he's, you know, a guy. Does that make me gay now?"

"Why does what you're feeling have to be labeled?" Mac asked.

Jack looked even more confused.

"Jack," Mac continued. "I struggled with the same thing when I discovered I was in love with Brad. Luckily I was open enough to realize that Brad and I had something special, and I wanted to explore it. I was scared shitless, but in the end, it was so worth the struggle."

Mac looked back and smiled at Brad. "But to be truthful, if anything ever happened and we weren't together, I can't say without any doubt that I would be with another guy. Maybe I'd meet another girl. After all, I was happily married to Lindsey for all those years, so why couldn't I choose another girl? My relationship with Brad has taught me that if you're open to it, it's more about the person you connect with and not so much about whether they are male or female."

"Well put," Brad whispered.

Jack seemed to lighten up a little, and even tried to force out a smile.

"Now I have a question," Brad said. "And this is very important, so I want you to consider your answer very carefully before you say anything."

Jack rolled his eyes and frowned, but gave Brad his undivided attention.

"Do you have real feelings for Dax, or are you simply curious about what it's like to have sex with a guy?"

Jack opened his mouth to speak and Brad raised his hand to stop him. "I said to think about your answer before you speak."

Jack closed his mouth. After a few minutes he said, "Can I speak now?"

"Only if you have a truthful answer," Brad responded.

Jack was looking out over the bow into the distance when he spoke. "I would be lying if I said I wasn't curious about sex with a guy. But I don't think I'm curious enough to actually do it if I didn't feel something for the guy."

Mac piped up, "That's good, because it's not fair to Dax if you're just giving him a trial run. I see the way he looks at you when he thinks no one is looking, and I feel certain he's experiencing some real feelings."

"See, that bothers me too," Jack proclaimed. "Why me? I'm nothing special. He's hot as hell. God, when he looks at me with those big, doe eyes I go weak in the knees and lose myself in him."

"That's a good thing, isn't it?" Brad asked.

"I guess," Jack said. "But I've never felt that way about anyone before. I think I could seriously fall in love with that man." Jack held out his trembling hands. "Look at me. I'm shaking like a leaf."

Brad and Mac looked at each other with a knowing smile. Jack was now starting to fidget.

"You don't think I know that I could hurt Dax? If it wasn't for that reason, I'd have jumped his bones last night," Jack admitted. "I know there's no turning back once I cross that line."

"Why, Jack Cameron, you're not the big lug we thought you were," Mac said. "You do have a conscience."

"Very funny, Mac."

"Just go for it, Jack," Brad said. "By the way you're acting and talking about Dax, I'd say you're a goner anyway."

"Holy shit," Jack said. "Don't say that, not yet."

Silence filled the fly bridge until it was broken by the sound of a squawking radio.

"Dax to bridge."

Brad and Mac noticed how Jack's eyes brightened when he said, "Bridge here. Hey, Dax."

"Hey, Jack. Dona and I have looked over our photos, as well as the video from the ROV, and we have a few points of interest under the surface to investigate."

"That's great," Jack replied. "You guys ready to suit up?"

"Give me ten minutes," Dax replied. "I want to prepare a couple of low-impact explosives to take down with us."

"Hell yeah!" Jack said. "Let's go blow some shit up."

"Don't get too excited, Jack," Dax said. "There's one little spot at the base of the mast that should reveal a dedication plaque, if it's even still there. But I'm sure, if it is there, that it'll be covered with a hundred years of sea growth and coral. If that turns up nothing, I've located a spot where the hull should be pretty thin and maybe we can penetrate it to get a better look."

"Now you're talking," Jack replied. "I'll meet you on deck in ten. Bridge out."

Dax laughed out loud and said, "Base out."

"So we're good?" Mac asked.

"Yep, real good," Jack said. "I think it's time to take a big leap of faith."

They smiled and made their way down to the deck to suit up for their last dive of the day.

AS THEY started their descent, Dona took the lead and headed for the wreck. Jack followed with a salvage bag of tools, Dax closely behind him with the lightweight explosives. When they got to the base of the mast, as Dax had expected, the area was covered with coral. He strategically placed the explosives at the base of the mast and told Jack and Dona to clear the area. When the three divers were together and safely away from the strike zone, Dax gave the "all clear" and "okay to detonate" to Brad and Mac up on deck. With everyone safely out of the area, Brad pressed the "detonate" button on the receiver.

Brad and Mac felt the rumble more than heard the explosion, but eventually saw a large water bubble appear at the surface. Dax, Dona, and Jack stayed clear for several minutes, allowing the explosion to settle and the coral and growth to sink back down to the bottom. As the water started to clear, they began to make their way back to the wreck. Dona was the first to reach the area, with Dax and Jack on her heels. The explosives had done a good job of cracking open the growth, but there was still a little clearing to do to get to the base of the mast.

Dona and Jack removed large crowbarlike tools from the bag and started scraping the surrounding area. Dax grabbed a smaller tool very similar to the ones Dona and Jack were using, but he went straight to work on the strike zone. Minutes later they all heard the "Hell, yeah!" from Dax and turned in his direction. Dax was grinning like a possum through a screen door, a look Dona knew all too well. Jack wasn't sure, but he had a good idea of what was happening. They gathered around Dax as he pointed to what was left of a fully intact brass plaque. He read out loud for everyone to hear:

"Eighteen Hundred and Seventy-One. Christened the *Anna Wyoming*, Camden Shipyard, Camden, New Jersey."

"Hell yeah!" Dax yelled again as he grabbed Jack and Dona, and they all bumped their full face masks together. Dona documented their find by taking several shots of the plaque with her underwater digital camera. Meanwhile, up on deck, Brad and Mac were screaming at the top of their lungs as well.

When the divers surfaced, Brad helped Dona up onto the swim platform. As Jack and Dax waited their turn, they threw their masks up on deck and hung on to the back of the boat. Jack grabbed Dax behind the neck and brought him in for a long, passionate kiss.

When the kiss ended, Jack said, "Congratulations, baby," and rested his forehead against Dax's. Dax smiled and said, "Thanks, Captain, and to you too." They heard the sound of someone clearing their throat and looked up to see Dona, Brad, and Mac standing there with their hands on their hips, smiling.

"Sorry," Jack said. "I couldn't help myself."

"What are you apologizing for, Jack? Those were my lips, and I sure as hell liked it."

Jack broke out into a broad, satisfied smile and looked up at the three sets of eyes staring down at them. "Never mind," he said, and they all laughed.

The team quickly shed their dry suits and stowed their equipment so they could get the *Lindsey C* underway and back to the dock in Skagway to start the process of staking their claim. Within an hour, the divers were in dry clothes and the gear was securely stowed. Jack pressed the "up" button on the windlass anchor winch, and the motor hummed as it slowly pulled the anchor back to the surface. When the anchor was secure, Jack pointed her bow toward Skagway.

Dona went below to download her photos and further document the day's activities, and Brad and Mac went to the galley to throw some food together. Back on the bridge, Dax sat in one of the captain's chairs while Jack checked the weather and plugged the coordinates into the GPS for the port of Skagway. When the autopilot was set, Jack sat back in his chair and looked at Dax. Jack stuck out his hand and Dax slowly slipped his hand into Jack's.

"You're incredible," Jack said. "I'm sorry it's taken me so long to come around to admitting that."

"Jack, this is all new to you, I get that. So don't be so hard on yourself."

"I just never thought I was gay," Jack admitted. "But Brad and Mac convinced me that whatever I am or we are doesn't have to have a title. Are you okay with that?"

"Okay with what, not saying we're boyfriends or lovers or life partners or husbands? Sure, I'm fine with that because, right now, we're none of those things."

"But...?" Jack asked as he leaned over and brushed his lips ever so slightly against Dax's. Dax gently kissed him back, but broke the kiss after just a few moments.

"But I do have one request, Jack," he said.

Jack tilted his head with a concerned look. "What's that?"

"You don't have to define our relationship to anyone right now, because we really don't have a relationship, but if this thing turns into something serious and we commit to one another, you can't pass me off as a buddy. If this is going to work, you can't be embarrassed of me or our relationship."

"Deal," Jack said, with relief in his voice. "We may not have a defined relationship this very second, and I won't speak for you, but as Brad and Mac pointed out to me earlier, when it comes to you, they think I'm already a goner."

Dax smiled, and those beautiful, lazy doe eyes captured Jack's heart yet again.

"And you know what, I think they're right."

"But I've got one more thing to say," Jack said.

"What's that?" Dax asked.

"Please give me a little time to get used to this arrangement. Knowing me, I will do my very best to mess this up, so you'll need to be patient with me."

Dax nodded, and then smiled and said, "Now shut up and kiss me."

Jack got out of his chair and stood in front of Dax's seat. Dax spread his legs, and Jack stepped in a little closer. He looked directly into Dax's beautiful hazel eyes as he ran his right hand through his silky, dark hair and cupped the back of his neck. He slipped his left hand in around Dax's waist and leaned in and gently kissed, then nibbled on Dax's neck. Dax moaned with pleasure, which Jack took as encouragement and continued the sensual assault. As Jack rubbed the back of Dax's head, he slowly moved up to kiss Dax's ear.

"You smell so good," Jack whispered, "Masculine and woodsy. I've never been this intimate with a man, but do all men smell this good?" Jack pulled back and looked at Dax, waiting for an answer.

"Are you serious?" Dax said.

"Yes, I am. If I'm going to be involved with a man, shouldn't I know these things?"

Dax thought for a moment and then conceded. "Okay, I don't want you smelling any other men, but yes, in my experience, every man has a scent that's uniquely his."

"I have a scent?" Jack asked.

"Yep. It's wonderfully musky with just a hint of sandalwood. It must be the soap you shower with or maybe the cologne you wear, but either way, it drives me absolutely crazy."

"Good to know," Jack said. "Absolutely crazy, huh?"

"Abbbbsolutely crazy."

Chapter *8*

IT WAS close to seven-thirty that night when the *Lindsey C* pulled into port. The sun was just starting to set, and the scene before them was breathtaking. As the sun hung just above the horizon, the sky was absolutely beautiful. Shades of purple and pink, orange and red, a few really dark blotches, and a bit of yellow were reflected off the water. Dax and Jack were still on the bridge, now joined by Brad and Mac, while Dona watched the grandeur of the sinking sun from the bow. As they inched along at idle speed, they all froze to take in the breathtaking sight. Just as the evening sun dipped below the horizon, the colors turned to rusts and reds, with a hint of fuchsia and a whimsical gold lining.

Jack guided the boat into his normal slip, and after the boat was secured, everyone met in the galley to decide on a plan. Dona suggested that Mac could fly her and Dax to Juneau at first light and the rest could stay behind and provision the boat for the next trip. But Mac assured her that they had plenty of provisions on board and they could shop during the waiting period while they awaited salvage permit approval. He also suggested that since he was trained to fly on instruments, they could all go to Juneau together that night, find a hotel room, have nice, long, hot showers, a late celebratory dinner, and be at the State Building first thing in the morning.

Dax voted for that idea because, secretly, he wanted the opportunity to be with Jack in a nice hotel room. Everyone else seemed excited about the long, hot shower and dinner in a restaurant. So in the end, they all agreed that they would get going ASAP.

Dona and Dax packed all the charts, photos, video, daily logs, and anything else they thought they might need and took it with them to prove that they'd truly found the *Anna Wyoming*. Brad and Mac's floatplane was secured nearby, and they all piled in and made the ninety-one mile flight to Juneau.

They safely touched down and took a cab downtown to find a hotel. It was nearing eleven o'clock when they located the State Building on West 9th Street and continued down the block until they came to the Juneau Hotel. They paid the driver, unloaded their bags, and walked toward the front desk. Brad and Mac were first to get there and stepped up to the counter. Jack, Dax, and Dona stood behind the velvet rope and formed a line to check in. Brad and Mac offered to let Jack bunk in with them, and he took them up on their offer. They reserved their room pretty quickly and headed straight for the hotel bistro, to see if they could get a table while Dax and Dona finished reserving their room. The restaurant was about to close, but allowed them in if they agreed to order quickly and not linger after their meal. Dona joined them shortly, but Dax was still standing at the front desk talking to the hotel clerk. They waited at the bar while the waiter set a large corner booth for them.

"So much for our celebratory meal," Jack mumbled as he wondered what was keeping Dax.

He didn't have to wonder long because when he turned around, Dax was standing right next to him. "There will be plenty of time for celebration," Dax said as he winked at Jack and rubbed the outside of his fingers across Jack's cheek.

Jack leaned into Dax's touch and purred like a kitten. Then he suddenly remembered where they were. He froze and looked around to make sure no one had seen the public display of affection. He quickly felt his entire body tense as panic filled his brain, and his first instinct was to swat Dax's hand away and bolt. But instead, remembering what he'd promised Dax earlier that day, he fought the fear, took a deep breath, and willed himself to calm down.

Dax had felt more than saw the moment Jack realized what was happening, and watched the panic as it overtook him. He also felt Jack fighting the urge to push his hand away. His heart skipped a beat in anticipation of the rejection surely to follow. But then Jack smiled that soft smile that always melted his heart, and he knew it was all okay. Brad, Mac, and Dona watched silently, as if taking bets in their heads on whether Jack would bolt or not, but he quickly relaxed and let it go when the moment had passed.

They enjoyed a quick dinner and a few glasses of wine, then all agreed that it had been a long, productive day and it was time to turn in. The State Building opened at eight-thirty, so they planned to meet for breakfast at seven o'clock. Dona was the first to give in to the exhaustion. She stood and said, "Good night. I'll see you guys in the morning."

"Good night, sis," Dax said.

"Have a good night, Dona," Jack said.

Mac and Brad said, "Wait for us. We'll ride up with you."

They stood and turned to Jack. "Will we see you tonight, Jack?" Mac asked.

Jack was caught a little off guard by the question, but quickly bounced back and looked over at Dax.

"I don't know. Dax, will I be seeing Mac and Brad later tonight?"

Dax felt like a deer caught in the headlights. He thought about the question for a second, turned beet red and said, "It's up to you, Jack, but if it were my call, I would say no, you won't see the guys tonight."

Jack smiled and squeezed Dax's thigh under the table. "Okay then, gentlemen, have a nice night, and I'll see you at breakfast."

Dona just smiled and turned toward the elevator.

Dax said, "Good night, guys." And Jack smiled shyly as the three of them walked away from the table.

Dax and Jack debated on another glass of wine, but in the end they decided not to indulge, as neither wanted a hangover to go with their six o'clock wake-up call.

Dax paid the check, and they got up to leave. Jack had left bars and restaurants many times in the past with his buddies and had never felt weird or self-conscious, but this time was different. He hadn't

planned on having sex with any of those guys. He blushed all the way
out of the restaurant and took a breath when he thought he was home
free. But then they had to pass the front desk, and although no one
stared or paid them any mind, he felt like everyone knew he was going
up to have his cock sucked by a man for the first time, and God only
knew what else.

They stepped up to the elevator, and Dax glanced at the room
number written on his key card—eight-twenty-two. He pressed the
"call" button on the elevator panel and looked up at the display over the
doors. A couple of seconds later, the elevator doors opened. Dax bent
over and made a wide, sweeping motion into the elevator as he held the
doors open. He whispered, "Your chariot has arrived, sir."

Jack smiled, and they stepped into the brass and mirrored elevator
and pressed the number eight on the panel.

The doors slowly closed. "Eight floors to go," Dax said. "I think
that's enough time for one really good kiss."

Dax dropped his bag and opened his arms as Jack did the same
and nervously stepped into them. He tilted his head upward, and before
he could say anything, Dax took his lips. Softly at first, then with a
sense of urgency Jack had rarely experienced. They were still kissing as
the bell dinged and the elevator slowly came to a stop. The doors
opened and Dax mumbled through the kiss, "I do believe we've
arrived." They picked up their bags and smiled again as they stepped
out of the elevator and went in search of their room. When they located
their home for the night, Dax swiped the keycard and watched the light
on the door handle go from red to green as the door latch released, and
they entered the room.

Much to Jack's surprise, the room was far from your typical hotel
room. *Well I'll be damned, he reserved a suite.* Dax flipped on the
light, and Jack saw that they were standing in a marbled foyer. To the
left was a powder room, and straight ahead was a parlor or sitting room.
Jack dropped his bag and whistled as he walked into the next room.
Much to his surprise, there was an ice bucket with a chilled bottle of
Veuve Clicquot champagne, along with two flutes sitting on the wet bar
in the corner. He walked to the next door and stuck his head in as he
checked out the bedroom.

Jack whistled. "Pretty sure of yourself," he said with a teasing smile.

"You mean the Veuve?" Dax asked.

"Among other things," Jack responded.

"The Veuve is a tradition that I've had for the last five years," Dax explained. "I find a wreck, I have a bottle of Veuve. The other things, well, let's just say I had my fingers crossed."

Dax stepped up to Jack and wrapped his arms around his waist. "Besides, I had no idea what was going to happen tonight, but either way, I knew the champagne and a suite couldn't hurt."

Jack looked a little confused.

"I mean, on the one hand, if you said yes and spent the night with me, I thought the suite and the champagne would be nice, romantic touches. And on the other hand, if you turned me down, I'd have someplace nice to cry and something to dull the pain of rejection. So either way, I thought it was a good idea."

Jack shook his head in amazement. "Dax Powers, you never cease to amaze me."

"And I hope I never stop amazing you," Dax said as he brushed his lips over Jack's. "How about opening the bubbly while I pee?"

"Sure."

When Dax came out of the bathroom, Jack handed him a tall, thin glass of champagne.

They touched their glasses together and Dax said, "To us and the *Anna Wyoming*."

"Cheers," Jack whispered.

"About us," Dax said.

Jack tilted his head and looked up at Dax.

"Listen, Jack, before anything happens between us, I've got to tell you that I'm pretty certain that my feelings for you are the real deal."

Jack opened his mouth to speak, and Dax placed his finger on Jack's lips.

"Please let me get through this. I've been falling for you since the day I walked onto your boat. The day we met, you thought my inability to speak was just me being rude, but in truth, I was so stunned by everything about you that I really couldn't speak.

"Jack, I'm no prude. I've had boyfriends before, but I've never felt like this. Not even close. I know it's probably way too soon, but it doesn't matter. I'm going with my gut feelings here and following my heart. This connection I'm feeling is something I've never had with anyone else, and it scares the hell out of me."

Jack focused on the words coming out of Dax's mouth. Although he couldn't comprehend it, was Dax actually saying that he was in love with him? And was he in love with Dax? Jack didn't think he'd ever really been in love. His marriage had been short-lived and, in the end, he'd known that he really hadn't loved her. He'd had a few other relationships along the way, but nothing had ever felt quite like this. Somewhere in the back of his heart, he believed it *was* love he was feeling for Dax. Could he man up and say it? And what would happen when the expedition was over?

Then the fear set in. Would Dax just leave him?

As soon as Dax finished speaking, silence filled the room. Dax could see the storm brewing behind Jack's beautiful blue eyes. But was the brewing storm caused by doubt, passion, or love?

"Jack, say something, anything."

Unable to control his emotions, Jack started to tremble. Dax put his glass on the table and took Jack's and did the same. He then took both of Jack's hands and lifted them to his lips and kissed them. Jack closed his eyes and tried to calm himself down before he attempted to speak. He opened his mouth, but nothing came out. His heart just wouldn't tell his brain to tell his mouth what to say.

Dax took the struggle he'd seen in his eyes and his inability to speak as Jack's answer. Dax's eyes were watering up pretty fast, and as a single tear slipped out of his left eye, he gently kissed Jack's hands, released them, and looked at the floor.

"Never mind, Jack. On second thought, please don't say anything. I understand, and I promise that you won't have to worry about me for the rest of the expedition. When it's over, we can just go back to our old lives and forget this ever happened."

Words and sentences and feelings were all consuming Jack's thoughts at once. *Say something, you idiot,* he told himself, and "I have feelings for you too," rushed out of his mouth.

Dax didn't believe his own ears. He smiled and used his fingers to wipe the tears away. "Can you repeat that?" he asked.

Jack took a deep breath and calmly whispered, "I have feelings for you too, Dax Powers. And although I haven't had time to sort through them all, I'm pretty sure they're real."

Dax picked Jack up like he was a rag doll and spun him around the room until they both landed on the couch.

"Jack, I want you so badly."

Jack moaned and planted kisses all over Dax's face. He stopped suddenly. "But I've never done this before. What am I supposed to do?"

Dax smiled. "All you need to do is let me love you, and the rest will all come naturally."

Dax stood and offered his hand to Jack, and he accepted it and stood. Jack grabbed his glass of champagne and downed it in one gulp. Dax gave his glass to Jack and took the bottle with them as he led Jack into the bedroom. He filled both of their glasses before he put the bottle down and attacked Jack's waiting mouth. Dax had one hand around Jack's neck and the other holding his champagne while he slowly maneuvered Jack until the back of Jack's legs hit the bed. Dax gently urged him down onto the bed before he broke the kiss. Dax tried to take Jack's glass from him, but Jack again downed the champagne before he surrendered the glass.

Jack looked so scared and cute at the same time, Dax could hardly control himself.

"What do I do?" Jack asked.

"We just do what feels right," Dax said. "We don't have to get off. To me, it's more about making love than having sex, so no pressure."

"My God, Dax, I'm already hard as a rock for you."

Dax fluffed up the pillows at the head of the bed and whispered, "Scoot up and relax while I undress you."

Jack did as he was told, and Dax got to work slowly undressing him. He started by untying Jack's boat shoes and slipping them off, one by one. He slowly massaged Jack's feet, trying to get him to relax. He removed his socks and gently kissed the tips of his toes, then moved up to his shirt. He unbuttoned the cuffs of Jack's shirtsleeves and then the buttons. Jack sat up and Dax slid Jack's shirt over his shoulders and down his back. He reached down and grabbed the hem of Jack's white T-shirt and pulled it over his head. He'd seen Jack's muscular chest when they were getting their dive suits on, but it had never looked better than it did right now. Dax gently brushed his lips over Jack's as he slid his hand down to unbuckle Jack's belt and pants. Jack lifted his hips, and Dax slid his khaki pants down his gorgeous legs and finally off. He stopped for a second to admire this sexy, handsome man lying in his bed.

Jack felt very exposed, lying there in nothing but his boxer briefs. He opened his eyes to see Dax looking at him with lust and desire, and it excited and scared him at the same time.

"This isn't fair," Jack said, leaning up on his elbows and looking at Dax, still completely dressed. "You still have your clothes on."

"No problem," Dax said as clothes started to fly. Within seconds he was stripped down to his boxers and lying in bed next to Jack.

Dax started with a nibble to Jack's ear that caused an immediate, even surprised moan. He licked down Jack's neck, gently nipping as he went. He wrapped his mouth around one of Jack's nipples, licking and gently biting, causing Jack to gasp.

"My God, Dax, you feel so good."

"Shhhhhh...."

Dax licked the trail of strawberry blond hair that ran down Jack's abs and past his navel. He tasted a smorgasbord of salt and sweat mixed in with Jack's wonderfully musky scent. Jack was simply delicious, and the taste of his skin sent pulses of electricity from Dax's tongue to his brain and then directly to his rigid dick. He traced up the other side of Jack's tight stomach and chest until he reached the other nipple. He gave it the same attention he'd given the first, and Jack was moaning and gasping as he whispered Dax's name over and over.

The sound of Jack's voice whispering his name was enough to make Dax come without even a touch, but he knew he had much more to show Jack. He wanted Jack's first sexual experience with a man to be the best he'd ever had. In addition, he wanted him to feel sensations he'd never felt before or even knew existed.

Dax traced his tongue back down Jack's chest and stomach toward the bulging tent in his underwear. He'd seen the outline of Jack's dick through the tight bathing suit he'd worn under his dry suit and knew he was very well endowed, but it wasn't until he placed his hand on it, through Jack's underwear, that he knew just how large it was. Dax moved his mouth further down Jack's torso until he reached the waistband of Jack's underwear. He continued down and slipped his mouth over Jack's still-clothed dick. Jack gasped and called his name when Dax slid his teeth over his erection. Dax slowly slid Jack's underwear down to his knees and then to his ankles and finally off, never once taking his eyes off of the prize.

Jack's dick was the most beautiful dick he'd ever seen. It was perfectly shaped and larger than he'd expected for Jack's height. It was thick and long and held a certain air of magnetism, and it stood there at attention, waiting to be admired. He looked from Jack's dick to his eyes and to his dick again and thought he had died and gone to heaven.

"Dax!" Jack shouted when Dax swallowed the head and most of the length of Jack's dick in one gulp. He applied a tight suction and began a slow, steady bob, gradually taking more and more until he could feel Jack's dick striking the back of his throat.

"Oh my God! Dax, that's gonna make me cum!"

Dax slowed down and backed off, then looked up at Jack. "You like?"

"Oh, yeah," Jack replied. "If you don't slow down, I'm gonna cum in record time."

"Okay by me. I like breaking records."

Dax returned his mouth to Jack's cock and swallowed his entire length this time in one gulp.

"Oh my God!" Jack shouted as he shot his load into Dax's warm, waiting mouth. Dax quickly licked and gulped to savor as much as he could of Jack's unique flavor. It had been quite some time since Dax had tasted another man's load, but he wanted to savor every drop of this one as it was coming from Jack, *his* Jack. Dax drained every bit of cum he could out of Jack's semi-erect cock and then released it from his mouth. He pushed himself up to straddle Jack and smiled as a thought came to mind. *I wonder how Jack would react to the taste of his own cum in my mouth?* Before Jack knew what hit him, Dax was kissing him fiercely, sliding his tongue in and around Jack's warm and sensuous mouth. When the kiss ended and Dax sat back, he watched Jack and waited for a sign.

Jack smacked his lips together. "That's so weird," he said. "I've never tasted my own cum, or anyone else's, for that matter."

"And?" Dax asked.

Jack reached up and cupped his hand behind Dax's neck and pulled him in ever closer and devoured his mouth. Jack's cock was getting hard again very quickly, and Dax could feel it against his own.

"Dax," Jack whispered. "I want to take care of you, but I'm not sure how good I'll be at it."

"It doesn't matter how good you are at it, Jack, the fact that you want to try can just as easily push me over the edge."

Jack rolled over on top of Dax and started nibbling at his neck. He worked his way down, just as Dax had done to him, and caressed his chest and nipples. He encircled Dax's nipples with his tongue one by one until Dax was arching off the bed. Jack took this as a good sign and continued his romantic assault.

"God, Dax, you smell so good, I just can't get enough of you."

Desperate to sample every inch of Dax's muscular body, Jack feasted on him until every part of Dax had been nibbled on, lightly bitten, or kissed into submission.

In the past, Dax had always been the aggressor and more dominant lover, but with Jack, he plunged into a state of abandon, giving himself completely to his lover and savoring the realization that this was the first time Jack had ever explored the strength, warmth, and hard body of another man. Dax was so lost in this man that, at this particular moment, Jack could take everything he had to offer and Dax would give it gladly.

Jack slid down the length of Dax's lean and muscular body and stopped when his fingers reached the waistband of Dax's boxers. He hesitated for only a second when he slid them off and tossed them to the floor. He studied Dax's rock-hard erection as if seeing a dick for the first time. Dax's dick was a tiny bit longer than his and just as thick, and he felt a quick sense of pride that he could compete with his lover in any dick contest. He dropped his head and hesitantly tasted the precum leaking from Dax's bulbous head. The taste was bitter and sweet and pure Dax, and he'd never tasted anything so good. He tentatively took the head of Dax's dick into his mouth. It was soft and smooth and warm, and although the sensation was foreign, it wasn't at all unpleasant. He remembered what it had felt like when Dax was swallowing him, and he wanted to give Dax the same sensation. He slowly moved his mouth up and down in small motions, getting completely used to the feeling. He quickly picked up steam and moaned as he forced his mouth down the entire length of Dax's cock. He immediately gagged and choked and backed off just a little to catch his breath, but he wouldn't stop. Dax deserved better than that. His persistence finally won out, and he was soon moving with a vengeance. Although his technique wasn't great, he more than made up for it with his enthusiasm.

Dax looked down and almost came at the sight of Jack's lips wrapped around his cock. Jack looked up, and when their eyes met, Dax could see a whole new world opening up for Jack. Jack looked very pleased with himself and proud of what he was accomplishing. It made Dax's heart pound, and before he could stop himself, he said, "Make love to me, Jack. I want to feel you inside of me."

Jack stopped, and Dax's cock slipped out of his mouth. "Did I hear what I just thought I heard?" Jack asked.

"Jack, don't make me say it again. I want your first time with me to be really special, and I want to remember this night for the rest of our lives."

"Dax," he whispered, "it already is more special than you can ever know. Nothing else has ever come close to being as good as this. You're amazing."

"Jack, in the top of my bag is my shaving kit. In there you'll find condoms and lube."

Jack hopped out of the bed with a new purpose. He located Dax's duffel bag and found the shaving kit. He retrieved the condoms and bottle of lube and scrambled back to position himself between Dax's open legs. Dax could see Jack's sudden hesitance, and remembered this was Jack's first time having anal sex with a man. "Don't worry, you won't hurt me if you take it easy and start slowly."

Jack spread Dax's legs wider as Dax slowly lifted his ankles and rested them on Jack's broad shoulders. He could feel his face blushing in the dimly lit room. Dax rarely bottomed, and he felt extremely vulnerable, but he wanted Jack. He wanted to feel Jack inside him, and above all, he wanted the strong emotional connection he felt to also be a physical one. "Once you're inside me, you can lose yourself. That's what's so great about having sex with a guy—we won't break."

Jack looked shy and scared, but did as Dax instructed. Jack squeezed lube on his fingers and gently touched Dax's waiting hole. He rubbed the lube around the hole and slowly began to penetrate Dax. Dax moaned with anticipation, which drove Jack crazy. Jack slowly worked his finger in and out, one and then two, until Dax was comfortable and relaxed. Jack positioned the head of his dick at Dax's entrance and gently pushed his way inside. Still not sure how this could not be hurting Dax, he stopped just as the head slipped inside.

Dax used his hands to help gently guide Jack along as he accepted what Jack was offering.

"Hold it there for just a second," Dax said, "just until I get used to the feeling."

As Dax took a deep breath and relaxed, he began to open for Jack. Jack sensed the change as Dax instructed him to move. Dax flinched with a slight flash of pain, but he soon adjusted to the incredible feeling of fullness as Jack began to move, very slowly at first, then picking up his momentum.

"Oh God, Jack, you feel so good. Please don't stop, just keep moving."

"This is incredible, Dax. You're so goddamn tight I can hardly stand it. Are you sure I'm not hurting you?"

"The only thing hurting me is you holding back. Just fuck me, and fuck me hard," Dax pleaded.

Jack plunged to the hilt inside Dax's rarely penetrated ass, causing Dax to gasp for air and raise his legs even higher, trying to get as much of Jack as he could. Jack increased the speed and intensity like someone who knew exactly what they were doing. It may have been his first time fucking a man, but Jack knew how to fuck, and Dax was close to losing control. He felt exploding heat and saw blinding flashes of light before his eyes and heard angels sing as the passion built between him and Jack. With every thrust, Dax was crying out with a need for Jack he'd never experienced with anyone else.

Sure, Dax had bottomed a few times, but he'd never really enjoyed it. It was different with Jack. Jack was touching his heart with every thrust, and he hungered for more.

"Oh, Jack, please, never stop ever. Fuck me forever. It's never, ever felt like this with anyone else."

"Dax, I'm there, can't hold back. Oh shit, Dax, I'm coming!"

Feeling Jack cum inside him with such intensity, Dax lost it too. He felt the burn start at the base of his balls and build until he came, harder than he could ever remember. Dax shot his first blast, which landed on his cheek, and the next, on his chin. The remaining shots hit his chest and abdomen. He could not remember having enjoyed a man's dick inside him more than this man's. The surge of ecstasy went on long after he came, and he didn't want to move, ever.

Jack looked at Dax, with cum dripping down his face, as they both gasped for breath. At that moment, Dax looked beautiful and vulnerable and like everything Jack thought he would ever need for the rest of his life. He opened his mouth to tell Dax that, but all that came out was a hoarse, raspy whisper.

"Dax," he forced. "It's never been like this with anyone, ever. Never thought it could feel this good."

"Me too, Jack, me too," Dax said as he used his tongue to wipe the cum off of his chin. He noticed how Jack watched his every move and looked both shocked and turned-on by the sexy demonstration.

"What?" Dax asked.

"How does it taste?"

"See for yourself," Dax offered.

"Can I?"

Dax nodded, and Jack slowly readjusted his position to get to Dax's cheek. In the process, he slid out of Dax, and Dax moaned as he felt the immediate sense of emptiness at Jack's withdrawal. Jack threw the used condom in the little trashcan by the bed and turned back to Dax. Dax instinctively reached out, not wanting to break the connection as Jack settled in next to him, leaning up on one elbow and cocking an eyebrow. *Here goes.* He stuck his tongue out and tasted Dax's seed, hesitantly at first, then smacked his lips together to fully taste the flavor and swallowed.

"Um," he said, "a little salty, a little bitter, and a little sweet, just like you. I like it." He surprised Dax by licking his face and chest clean, this time with a vengeance and a purpose.

When Dax was totally clean, Jack licked his lips and laid his head on Dax's chest.

"You know, Jack, this is not my first time at the rodeo, but man, I got to tell you that nothing has ever come close to this. I'm usually the guy on top, but if this is what I've been missing all my life, then, Mr. Cameron, your bottom has arrived, and welcome aboard."

Jack lifted his head off of Dax's chest. "What do you mean, you don't bottom?"

"Some guys prefer to top and some to bottom, and some even like to do both. As I'm sure you're well aware, I have a little bit of a control issue."

"Ya think?" Jack asked with a smile.

Dax jabbed Jack in the ribs. "Bottoming requires a person to relinquish control to a certain extent."

"So you did something you don't particularly care for, just for me?" Jack asked.

"Yeah, I really wanted your first time to be special and really good. But don't get me wrong, I loved it, and I'll bottom for you anytime. I've never cum that hard before."

"Dax, this has been so special. And that's because it was with you. We could have stopped at any time, and I would have been happy just to be next to you, but feeling your warmth while I was inside you, that was like an awakening for me. I've never felt so close or intimate with anyone ever before, and I think you've ruined anyone's chances of ever topping that."

"I hope no one ever gets a chance to try and top it, ever. I want you all to myself, I love you, Jack Cameron."

Jack snuggled tightly against Dax and again used his chest as a pillow. Dax ran his hand through Jack's long, silky locks, not admitting to himself how disappointed he was that Jack hadn't said he loved him as well. *Give him a break*, he thought. *After all, he's just had his first sexual experience with a man, and he probably needs time to digest all the emotions.*

They stayed in that position for several moments, content just to be touching each other and basking in their afterglow.

Jack lifted from his position and looked up to face Dax.

"I've never been in love before, Dax," Jack said.

Dax held his breath but didn't say a word, not sure of what was coming next.

"But if what I'm feeling right now is any indication of what love feels like, then I'm in way over my head."

Dax released his breath. "Jack, we've just taken a big step, and I don't want either of us to get hurt. And I know I've said this before, several times, but we've got to move slowly and make sure this is what you want."

"Come on, Dax. Give me a little credit. I'm not a kid here. Yes, I've never been in love, and yes, I didn't know I was gay, and yes, it took me a while to get used to the idea, but I know what I'm feeling. I know you're worried that this is just an infatuation for me, but it's not. This feels like the most real thing I've ever done. My God, it's life-changing, and I'm going through it with you."

"Okay, I get it. I know the high you're on right now. Hell, I'm right there with you, but there's a lot more to being in love with a man than just making love. I've been out of the closet forever and don't plan on going back in any time soon, and you've got to understand that you'll be outed just for being associated with me. Are you prepared for that?"

Jack was silent for a moment. He lifted his head again and gently kissed Dax's full lips. "If we're together, I'm ready for anything," he whispered.

Dax wrapped his arms around Jack and pulled him in even closer.

"Dax, we don't know each other very well, and you have no way of knowing this, but my parents are both dead, and Brad, Mac, Mac's daughter Zoe-Grace, and her husband Zachary are the only family I have left. Theirs are the only opinions I care about, and obviously they don't have a problem with this, therefore, neither do I. I love you too, and I don't care who knows it."

Dax smiled and said, "You win, Captain. I'd trust you with my life, so I guess I can trust you with my heart. Please don't break it."

It was very late when they made love for the last time that night and almost collapsed from exhaustion. Dax lay snuggled tightly behind a lightly snoring Jack, with the weight of the world on his shoulders.

I know I'm in love with Jack, but did I do the right thing by professing my love? By doing so, he gets thrown into this world that I'm not sure he's prepared for. This will change everything for him. And what about me—what if he decides that he doesn't want to be gay? Where does that leave me?

He struggled with his thoughts for another couple of hours. Totally defeated, he finally decided that what was going to happen was going to happen. He would stand by Jack and protect him with his life. And after that, putting his heart on the line was a small risk and he was willing to take it.

Sit back and hold on for the ride, Dax, was his last thought before he drifted off to sleep.

Chapter 9

DAX was forced out of his dream by the sound of a blaring alarm clock. He kept his eyes tightly closed, knowing that once he opened them, the magical night he'd just spent making love with Jack would be over. He wasn't ever going to be ready for that, so he pulled the covers up over his head and reached for Jack. Only when he felt an empty bed did he crack one eye and peer through. Jack was gone.

Fear made his internal alarm sound as loud as the damn alarm clock, but he tried to force it away. He knew he wouldn't be able to control the alarm in his head, so he reached back and slapped the snooze to get rid of the one alarm he *could* control, but damn if it wouldn't stop. Suddenly, the bathroom door opened, and Jack stepped out wearing nothing but a towel. Dax blinked his sleep-filled eyes to get a better look. *God, he's gorgeous*, he thought as he stared at the vision in front of him.

"Are you going to answer that?" Jack asked.

Confused, still half-asleep, and drooling over this manly vision, Dax didn't have a clue of what Jack was talking about, "Answer what?"

"The phone, you goofball."

Now it all made sense; it wasn't the alarm clock, it was the phone.

"Oh, the phone." Dax reached for the ringing phone. "Sorry, I was distracted by a handsome man. Hello!"

"It's about time you answered," Dona said. "Please tell me you're not doing it."

"Unfortunately not," Dax replied.

"Oh good. Are you boys ready to go?"

"Not quite. Jack just got out of the shower, and I'm about to hop in. We'll meet you downstairs for breakfast in about fifteen minutes."

"Okay, hurry. We want to be there when they open, get this done, and get back to the boat by this afternoon."

"The sooner you let me off the phone, the sooner we can be ready."

With that statement, Dax heard a click. He put the phone down and stuck a hand out to Jack. Jack sat beside him on the bed and leaned in for a good-morning kiss.

As their lips met, Dax pulled away. "No fair," he said. "You've already brushed you teeth."

"Oh come on, it doesn't bother me."

"Nope," Dax said. "But be prepared. When I get out of the shower, you've got the biggest, sloppiest kiss coming your way."

Dax jumped out of bed and started toward the bathroom. When Jack stood, Dax rushed back, pulled Jack's towel off, and backed toward the bathroom door. He stopped in the doorway and looked at the naked vision of the man standing before him. Jack's handsome face and towel-dried, reddish-blond hair sat atop a set of broad shoulders. His massive chest was lightly sprinkled with blond hair that led down to a set of luscious abs that the term "six-pack" just wasn't enough to adequately describe. His long cock and beautifully shaped balls hung between two thick, muscular thighs that led down to great calves and slender feet.

Jack self-consciously watched as Dax studied him. He began to blush and finally asked, "What?"

"Just trying to figure out how I got so lucky, that's all."

Jack smiled with relief as Dax grabbed his bag and disappeared into the bathroom, shaking his head.

Ten minutes later Dax exited the bathroom dressed in a long-sleeved, yellow fleece sweatshirt over a red T-shirt and a pair of nicely fitting jeans.

"Wow, you look good enough to eat," Jack said as he stood there in almost the same type of outfit.

"We almost look like twins," Dax said as he opened his arms. "Come here, Captain, I owe you something."

Jack gladly walked over to his lover, and as they embraced, Dax pressed his full lips against Jack's and begged for entry. Jack welcomed him, and their tongues danced the dance as they shared their morning kiss.

They were interrupted by the phone ringing again. Without breaking the kiss, they sidestepped to the phone, and Jack picked up the receiver. He pulled his lips away from Dax's just long enough to say, "We're on our way."

He heard the caller sigh and hang up without saying a word.

"We better go, before we get in trouble," Jack said.

"Do we have to?" Dax pleaded.

"I don't know about you, but I don't think I want to take Dona on this early in the morning, do you?" Jack asked.

"Nah, I guess you're right. She can be a bull dyke when she wants to."

Jack howled with laughter.

After one last quick kiss they picked up their bags and made their way to the elevator. When the elevator door opened on the main floor, the gang was waiting for them. Catcalls and whistles filled the hotel lobby, followed by loud applause. Dax and Jack looked at each other, turned a horrible shade of red, and smiled. Jack pushed the button in the elevator, and the doors started to close. Mac stuck his foot in the doors to stop them, and they bounced back open. He grabbed Jack by the shoulders and kissed him right on the lips. Brad stepped in and did the same to Dax. Dona stood outside the elevator door, tapping her foot and smiling.

"Jack Cameron, you better not hurt my big brother," she said. She opened her arms and Jack stepped into them.

"I'll do my best," he said.

When they broke the embrace, she turned to Dax. "And the same goes for you, bro," she said as she embraced him next. "Now that you two have played *Hide the Willy*, can we get on with the expedition?" she asked.

They all laughed and walked to last night's bistro, now converted to a breakfast café. They got a table and ordered quickly. While they waited for their food to arrive, the table buzzed with conversation about the process for getting the salvage rights to the wreck.

Jack raised his hand just a little. "I have a question. I thought I read somewhere that salvage rights were requested in Federal Court, not at the local level."

"You're right," Dax said. "It used to be that way, but since the *Abandoned Shipwreck Act of 1987*, the US Government turned over rights of known and unknown shipwrecks to the respective states, to manage as they see fit."

"So, if all goes well, in the next week, we could have the paperwork we'll need to get the salvage started," Dona added.

"Got it," Jack said as the server started bringing their food to the table.

Jack and Dax had ordered a ton of food, and when their food arrived before anyone else's, the table was almost covered.

Dona looked at the amount of food on the table. "My God," she said. "I guess lovemaking can make for a pretty big appetite."

Everyone laughed again at Dax and Jack's expense, but they simply smiled sheepishly and dug in. Everyone ate pretty quickly when the rest of the food came. They paid the check and walked the block to the State Historic Preservation Office, located in the State Capital building.

When they reached the office, there was a female clerk standing at the counter. Dax and Dona approached and explained to her that they wanted to apply for a Rights of Salvage certificate for the wreck of the *Anna Wyoming*. She explained that she needed to gather the appropriate paperwork, and she would be right back. She disappeared into the back office and minutes later reappeared with a gentleman who introduced himself and explained he was the clerk in charge of giving out salvage permits. He handed them a stack of paperwork and explained that the paperwork needed to be completed in its entirety before the request could be considered.

They all took seats and divided the paperwork among them. It covered topics such as the research vessel, the crew, the wreck, Dax and Dona's experience, and a boatload of other information. They all completed what they knew and passed it along to the next person to do the same. When all the paperwork had made the rounds, every question had been thoroughly answered. Dax added the printed photos and videotape, and they were finished. He turned in the paperwork and returned to his seat as the clerk disappeared through a doorway.

"What happens next?" Brad asked.

"We wait," Dona said. "Once they review the paperwork and make sure we completed everything properly and they have everything they need, they'll tell us we can go, and they'll contact us when they make a decision. It normally takes a few days to a week, so we'll go back to Skagway and prepare the *Lindsey C* for the salvage."

Thirty-five minutes later, the male clerk appeared through the same door he'd used to exit, approached the counter, and looked at Dax.

"Mr. Powers," he said. "We have your salvage rights."

"What?" Dax said as he stood and made his way to the counter.

"You're all set," he replied.

"Are you sure? It usually takes a few days," he said.

"Yes, sir, I'm sure," he said. "Here is your Rights of Salvage certificate for the wreck of the *Anna Wyoming*."

Not wanting to rock the boat, Dax said, "Thanks, and you have a good day now." He turned and motioned with his head for the rest of them to follow him. He wanted everyone out of there before the gentleman realized he'd made a terrible mistake and tried to take the certificate back. They all followed his lead, very quickly, and no one spoke until they reached the lobby of the building.

Dona was the first to make a sound. "Dax, what do you make of that?"

"Don't know," Dax replied. "But it's very strange. We've never received Rights of Salvage on the same day, ever."

"What do you think it means?" Brad asked.

"Not sure," Dax replied. "But my guess would be that either someone made a mistake, or someone wants to know what's in that ship pretty badly. The only potential problem I can see is that if someone did make a mistake, our rights can be challenged in a court of law at any time."

"But we have the certificate," Jack said. "Doesn't that count for anything?"

"It certainly helps, but it can still be challenged."

"Anything can be challenged," Dona said. "I say we go for it."

"I agree," Jack said.

Brad and Mac looked at each other and nodded. "Not that it matters, but we do too," Brad said.

"Then it's official," Dax proclaimed. "You're all now treasure hunters."

"Yee doggy, Brad," Mac said. "We's treasure hunters."

"Darn tootin'," Brad replied.

WITH a new pep in their step, they exited the lobby into a glorious, Alaskan summer morning and decided to walk to the plane instead of hailing a taxicab.

When they reached the plane, Brad and Jack loaded the luggage while Mac filed a flight plan with the Harbor Authority. Thirty minutes later, they were airborne for Skagway.

While in flight, they decided that as soon as they landed, Jack, Dax, and Dona would head right to the boat, and Mac and Brad would secure the plane. Since they didn't have to wait for the permit, they would get a cab and go into town for more supplies. They also decided that they should try and depart Skagway no later than four that afternoon, which would give them plenty of time to get to the site, drop the hook, and get a good night's sleep before they started the salvage the next morning.

The weather was perfect for flying and the flight was beautiful and uneventful. They landed just after noon and everyone followed their assigned responsibilities.

Jack, Dax, and Dona walked back to the *Lindsey C* and stepped aboard. Approaching the companionway door, Jack saw that the door was slightly ajar and stopped dead in his tracks. He stuck his hands out by his side, palms back, and made a motion for Dax and Dona to stop.

"Something's not right," he whispered.

"What do you mean, something's not right?" Dona asked.

"I know I closed this door when we left," he said. "Stay here."

"I'm not letting you go down below alone," Dax said.

"Neither am I," Dona added.

"Fine," Jack said. "Just be careful."

Jack was the first one to see the condition of the salon. Every drawer was opened, emptied, and overturned. Most of his navigational charts and books were on the floor and the bookcases searched. Everything was removed from the storage compartments under the sofas and thrown everywhere as well.

"Get topside and take Dona with you," Jack whispered.

Seeing the condition of the salon, Dax said, "No. I'm not leaving you down here alone."

"Just do it, Dax, take care of Dona. I'll be fine."

"Fuck both of you," Dona whispered. "I don't need anyone taking care of me. Do you have a gun on this damn boat or do I have to kick some ass with my bare hands?"

"Oh hell," Jack huffed. "Leave it to me to go into business with Bonnie and Clyde."

He pulled *War and Peace* off of one of the shelves untouched by the intruders, opened it, and retrieved his forty-five, which was stashed in the hollowed-out shell of the book.

"Oh, good Lord," Dona said as she saw the gun. "I thought you were stopping to read a classic."

He removed the safety, and with Dax and Dona closely following, he slowly made his way toward the galley and forward cabins, listening for any sign that the intruders might still be on board.

When they reached the galley, as in the salon, every drawer was opened, emptied, and overturned, and pots and pans as well as silverware were strewn everywhere. Without stopping, Jack worked his way toward the sleeping cabins. Opening the first cabin door carefully with his gun pointed forward, he saw that all the drawers and closets there had been emptied and searched. The mattress was pulled off of the bed and lying on its edge, and the compartments underneath the mattresses were emptied and searched as well. They went from one cabin to the next, and they were all in the same condition. Lastly, he opened the forward cabin door to their makeshift home base. It was surprisingly untouched. It appeared to have been searched as well, but care had been taken not to disrupt the equipment, which didn't make sense to any of them. The three then made their way to the aft master cabin and it, too, was in the same condition as the others. But after a quick search, it appeared that the intruders were no longer on board, and the threat of danger was gone for the moment. Jack put the safety back on his forty-five and laid it on his desk.

His first glance was to his bedside table. The top drawer was missing, but he quickly scanned the small cabin and saw the overturned drawer lying near his bed. He lifted the drawer and a black, zippered Alaska Pacific Bank bag fell out and landed at his feet. He unzipped the bag and removed an untouched stack of cash. He lifted the cash to show Dona and Dax.

"Look what they missed," he said.

"Should we call the police?" Dona asked.

Dax was the first to speak. "It's Jack's call because it's his boat, but my vote would be no," he said. "Why bring any unwanted attention to the expedition?"

"I agree," Jack said. "And besides, nothing seems to be missing, so they'd most likely write it off as some random act by local kids."

"You're probably right," Dona said. "But it feels weird not doing anything."

"There's enough to do to just get this boat back in shape before we leave," Jack replied. "So let's get our butts in gear."

The three of them started the process of cleaning up the boat and putting things away. They each started with their own cabin, and then Jack took the galley while Dax and Dona took the salon. They didn't feel comfortable going through Brad and Mac's things, so they left their cabin for when they returned.

They were about halfway through when they heard two car doors close and Brad yell, "Helloooo, get your sorry asses out here and help us unload."

Jack went topside and was greeted by Brad handing him a cardboard box. He took the box and carried it down below. Brad and Mac followed with boxes of their own and stopped short when they saw the condition of the salon.

"What in the hell happened in here?" Mac asked.

"We had visitors," Jack said.

"What? Are you serious?"

"Oh yeah, we're serious!" Dax exclaimed. "And wait until you see your cabin."

"He's right," Dona said. "We've already put our cabins back together, but didn't feel comfortable going through your stuff."

"Lord only knows what kind of sex toys we would have found in there!" Dax said.

"Very funny," Mac said.

Brad and Mac listened while Jack explained what they'd found when they returned to the boat.

"Those bastards better not have touched my underwear," Brad said. "That's just creepy."

"I know what you mean," Dona said. "But be prepared. I've thrown mine away, and I'm going back into town shortly to buy new ones."

"If they've touched ours…. I'm going with you," Brad said.

They all helped unload the car and finished putting everything away in the galley and salon. Brad and Mac retreated to their cabin to put it back together, and in just under an hour, the door flew open, and Brad emerged with a trash bag.

"But that's perfectly good underwear," Mac whined as he followed Brad to the trashcan. "My favorite boxers are in that bag. Can't we just wash them?"

"Nope," Brad said. He opened the lid, dropped the bag into the can, and brushed his hands together to signify the decision was made, and the job was done.

"Call me queer if you want to," he said. "But I'm not wearing underwear that some stranger's touched, and neither are you. Where's Dona?"

Very amused at the test of wills, Dax and Jack watched from the galley where Dax was cleaning vegetables and Jack was marinating steaks for dinner. "She's in her cabin," Dax said.

With everyone watching, Brad spun on his heels in a defiant move and tapped on Dona's door.

"You ready to make an underwear run?" he yelled through the door.

"I'll be ready in a minute," she responded. "Call a cab."

"Okay, I'll meet you topside," Brad said as he moved away from the door.

Mac followed Brad up the companionway and on to the bow and stood silent while Brad ordered a cab.

When Brad hung up the phone, they stood there looking out over the horizon.

"Look, Mac, I know you think I'm crazy, but I just hate the thought of someone touching our underwear. People touch our clothes all the time because we wear them on the outside, but our underwear is something private, just for you and me."

"Okay, okay I get it," Mac said. "Go buy us some new underwear."

Brad kissed Mac and said, "Thanks for understanding."

Mac took the kiss a little deeper as Dona appeared on deck.

"Get a room, you two," she said.

Mac stuck his tongue out at Dona. "You're just jealous," he said.

"Oh yeah, that's it. Brad, don't take this the wrong way, but I'm not buying what you boys are selling."

Mac and Brad smiled. "Yeah, we know," Brad said. "No hard feelings."

"Hey, Dona," Mac said. "Do you have a girlfriend?"

"Not at the moment," she replied. "This lifestyle doesn't leave much time for romance."

"The lifestyle didn't seem to stop Dax," Mac said.

"Yeah, but he's always been a bit of a whore," she said with a smile. "I'm really happy for them, but surprised at the same time."

"How so?" Brad asked.

"Jack is not his usual type," she explained.

"Really?" Mac said.

"Yeah, in the past he's always gone for the starry-eyed young boys who idolized him. But with Jack, it seems different. Hell, *he* seems different. I think Jack will be good for him."

"I sure hope so," Mac said. "Jack has really gone out on a limb here. We always thought he was gay, but he'd never admitted to it, or acted on it as far as we know."

"I've got a good feeling about this one, but only time will tell," Dona said as she grabbed Brad's hand. "Let's go, hotshot."

Brad kissed Mac on the cheek and said, "We won't be long."

"Remember, Jack wants to leave by four."

"Yes, dear," Brad yelled as he was being dragged off the boat. "We'll be back in plenty of time."

Mac watched Brad and Dona leave and then he headed down below to see if he could help with the preparations for dinner. When he reached the salon, Dax and Jack were sitting on the couch, discussing their unwanted guests. He glanced at the galley, and all the food preparation seemed to have been completed.

They both looked up when they heard Mac come through the companionway.

"Perfect timing," Jack said as he motioned for him to join them. "We just finished."

"Oh good," Mac said. "I thought I might have to help."

The three men shared a laugh and Mac said, "If you don't need me, I'll take the rental car around the corner and drop it off."

"I'll do that," Dax said.

"Want me to come with you?" Jack asked.

"Nah, I can handle it, but thanks."

"What were you guys talking about?" Mac asked before Dax had time to get up.

"About the break-in," Dax said. "We're pretty certain this wasn't a random act of vandalism."

Jack tapped his fingers on the end table as he offered his opinion. "Here's the way I see it, guys," he explained. "It seems to me that, if they were kids, they would have taken everything they thought they could sell and destroyed everything else on board, including the equipment."

"That makes sense," Mac added.

"But they didn't touch any of the equipment down below or on the bridge, and they didn't take the bank bag of cash in my cabin, which tells me they were looking for something in particular."

"Like maybe the coordinates to a wreck?" Dax asked.

"Precisely," Jack said.

"And since they didn't find what they were looking for on board," Dax said. "They wanted our equipment in good working order to lead them to it."

"You think someone's been following us?" Mac asked.

"That would explain a lot," Dax said. "Let's put the facts together. First, no one's been able to find this wreck for over one hundred years, yet we stumbled onto the coordinates under very odd circumstances. Secondly, the Rights of Salvage came way too easy. It was all but handed over to us on a silver platter. And lastly, someone came aboard and disrupted everything but the navigation and reconnaissance equipment. It all seems very odd to me."

"If someone is watching us, they want something," Jack said. "And I think that something is our gold," he added. "We really need to watch our backs from this point forward."

Mac jumped in, "But it's almost impossible to watch our backs when there's so much traffic on the Canal. Any number of boats coming and going could be watching us, and we would have no way of knowing."

"I guess we pay a little more attention," Jack said. "I think one of us should be on duty with binoculars, watching every vessel that passes. We can look up the registration at the United States Coast Guard Web site and start keeping a log. Anything out of the ordinary will stand out, and we can investigate each questionable vessel on a case-by-case basis."

"Sounds like a plan," Dax said.

"Now, can we talk about something else for a while? All this espionage crap is starting to freak me out," Mac said.

"Sure, what do you want to talk about?" Dax asked.

"How about you guys?" Mac asked.

Dax smiled at Jack, and he started to blush.

Dax thought Jack might like to talk to Mac alone, so he saw this as a good opportunity to take the car back. "I'll catch up with you guys later," he said.

He kissed Jack on the lips, stood, and headed up the companionway.

"Be careful, and watch your back," Jack said.

"I will," Dax replied.

"That was a hasty retreat," Jack said.

"Maybe he thought you and I might need to talk," Mac responded.

"Why would he think that?"

"Possibly because you had your first sexual experience with a man last night, and he thought you might want to talk about it?" Mac asked.

Jack thought for a moment, then shook his head. Before he could say anything, Mac continued.

"Come on, Jack, you must want to pick my brain about something? It wasn't that long ago that I was in your shoes, and I sure wished I'd had someone to talk to. Lord knows you were no help."

"Nope, I'm good," Jack said.

Mac looked crushed, and Jack immediately regretted his words.

"Look, Mac, I really appreciate it, but I really am good. I'm not having any second thoughts, and in fact, I think it was the first time that I've ever really made love."

"Are you saying you're in love with Dax?" Mac asked.

"I think so." Jack paused. "No, wait, I don't think so. I *know* that I'm in love with Dax." Jack smiled.

Mac stood, crossed the salon, and sat next to Jack. He put his arm around his shoulder and said, "Man, I wish you two the best. Dax seems to be a great guy, and well, I know you're a great guy, so this should work out just fine."

"Thanks," Jack said. "I really appreciate your support. And I'm sorry I wasn't there for you. You know, back then. In hindsight, I guess when I found out about you and Brad, it hit just a little too close to home."

"That's an understatement," Mac chuckled. "But all's forgiven. I love you, man."

"I love you too," Jack said as he looked uncomfortably at his watch. "It's almost four. I'm starting to worry about Brad and Dona," he said. Before he could say another word, their alone time was interrupted by a loud thump and the companionway door flying open.

"Awhoooore, I mean, Ahoy!" Brad said as they stumbled down the companionway carrying several shopping bags and giggling uncontrollably.

Jack and Mac looked at each other and smiled. "You two look like you've had a great time," Jack said.

"And it looks like you managed to get a little shopping done between cocktails," Mac added.

"Whaz yur point?" Dona slurred as she looked at Mac and poked him in the ribcage.

"Yeah, whaz it to ya?" Brad asked with a grin.

Dona giggled again.

Dax came in from returning the car and heard all the commotion. "What's this?" he asked. Brad and Dona were smiling wickedly.

"Heeeey there, bro," Dona said.

"It appears that these two had a great time shopping," Jack said.

"Looks that way," Mac added. "Come on, kids, how about we get you two down for a little nap before we shove off?"

Brad and Dona looked at each other, made a nasty face, and said, "Yuk," simultaneously.

"Okay, separate cabins," Mac said as he took Brad by the hand and led him to their cabin. Dax did the same with Dona, and once again quiet was restored to the small salon.

Jack sat there soaking up the quiet. So much had happened to him over a short period of time, and as he thought about it, he realized that he couldn't be happier. He was in love with Dax, and more importantly, Dax loved him. Dax joined him in the salon and snuggled into him with a gentle kiss. "Dona okay?" Jack asked.

"She's out like a light. She's not a big drinker, so I know she'll be bitter when she wakes up with a hangover."

Jack smiled. He pulled Dax closer to him and wrapped his arms around him tightly.

"You're a good brother," he said as he kissed his cheek.

"Ah shucks, Miss Daisy," Dax said with a smile. "But this doesn't make a dent in the amount of times she's done the same for me. I owe her big-time."

"Now it's my job to take care of you," Jack said.

"I like the sound of that," Dax replied.

"Me too," Jack said as he again looked at his watch. "I'd love to stay this way forever, but it's almost four-thirty, we'd better get underway."

Dax quickly kissed Jack on the cheek and yelled for Mac. Mac came into the salon with a huge smile across his lips.

"Everything okay?" Jack asked.

"He's all tucked in, sleeping like a baby. But not before he attempted to try on his new underwear for me. Every time he bent over to grab the underwear and pull them up over his knees, he fell onto the bed. After the third time, he finally gave up and passed out with them around his ankles. Not a bad sight, I must say."

They all chuckled and made their way on deck. Jack headed for the bridge, Mac to the bow, and Dax to the stern. They released the lines, secured the fenders, and minutes later, the *Lindsey C*'s side thrusters were inching her away from the dock. Dax joined Jack on the bridge, while Mac grabbed the binoculars and took an inconspicuous seat with an aft view. He jotted down the names as he watched several vessels immediately pull out of port behind them. Skagway was a large port with a lot of traffic, so it wasn't unusual for boats to follow one another in and out of port. Mac would keep a close eye out, and later look up each boat to see to whom and where it was registered.

Chapter 10

THE trip back to the wreck was uneventful, and soon they were dropping the hook and securing the boat for the night. Mac joined Dax and Jack on the bridge. He handed Jack the log book he'd started of the vessels coming and going during their journey. Jack looked over all the vessel names and identified many local fishing boats and crossed them off the surveillance list. Of course, someone could have chartered any number of those boats for the purpose of spying on them, but he personally knew the captains and considered them friends. None of the men would allow a reconnaissance charter without at least letting him know about it.

They all went below, and while Dax and Jack settled with the laptop at the banquette, Mac started preparing dinner. There were three boats that Jack didn't recognize as local, and he looked them up on the Coast Guard's Web site. Two of them were registered as fishing boats, about sixty feet in length, and were owned by Klondike Industries in Anchorage. The third vessel appeared to be about one hundred feet in length, was named "прогулочный катер," which loosely translated meant "pleasure boat," and was privately owned and registered to a man named Vladimir Kozlov. The hail port on the stern was Provideniya, Russia, which was a Russian port just across the Bering Sea. Because the vessel was registered in Russia, the Web site offered only the owner's name and hail port. They would keep a special eye out for this vessel if it crossed their paths again, and continue the reconnaissance until they were sure they weren't being followed.

Dona came out of her cabin and slowly maneuvered into the salon with one hand running along the wall for stability and the other holding her head.

"What time is it?" she asked.

Dax and Jack looked up from the reconnaissance list with similar smiles, while Mac smiled without looking up.

"A little after nine," Dax replied. "We were just about to call you for dinner."

"That reminds me, I need to try and get Brad out of bed as well," Mac said. "Keep an eye on the stove, will you, guys?"

"Sure thing," Jack replied.

"Dona, can I get you anything?" Dax asked.

"Not unless you can stop this throbbing headache," she said.

"Imagine if I hadn't forced you to take those two Advil earlier," Dax added.

"Wow, that's the last time I shop with Brad."

"Did he secure your arms behind your back and force-feed you those cocktails?" Dax asked.

"Very funny," she said as Mac came into the salon with Brad in tow. Brad looked as bad as Dona, and he smacked her on the butt as he passed.

"That's the last time I go shopping with you," he said.

"Me?"

"Yes, you," he shot back.

"Oh brother," Dona said as she rolled her eyes.

They both smiled and sat on the couch. Mac approached with four Excedrin and two glasses of water. They gladly accepted the offerings and quickly downed the drugs.

"Hey, Brad, I half-thought you were going to come out here with your new underwear around your ankles," Jack said. "I heard you had a little difficulty getting them on."

Brad looked at Mac with a pair of evil eyes and replied, "Very funny, Jack, but maybe later."

After the laughter quieted, Jack and Dax filled them in on the vessel reconnaissance and what they had found while Mac finished preparing dinner. As usual, during dinner they discussed the plans for the next day, and by the end of the meal Brad and Dona appeared to be feeling somewhat better. Everyone helped with the cleanup and all agreed it would be an early night, with so much on the agenda for tomorrow. Mac and Brad were the first to turn in, with Dona right behind them. Jack and Dax headed to the bridge, and while Jack verified that their position was holding, Dax used the night-vision binoculars to do a quick scan of the area. He saw nothing out of the ordinary and said, "Looks clear, you ready to call it a night?"

"I thought you'd never ask. I've been dying to get you in bed all day."

"All you have to do is ask, Captain, and I'm yours, anytime."

Jack softly kissed Dax and said, "Let's go."

Jack shut off the lights as they exited the bridge. If they had only stayed on the bridge for fifteen minutes more, they would have seen the "прогулочный катер" cruise by for its fourth time since they had dropped anchor earlier that evening.

JACK didn't wait until he reached the cabin. His lips were already covering Dax's by the time they'd reached the companionway. Their tongues explored as if their mouths were the entrance to their souls. When they reached the cabin, Jack was still devouring Dax's mouth. He opened the door, nudged Dax inside, and kicked it closed with his foot. He gently backed Dax up against the bed and in one fluid move pulled Dax's shirt over his head. Following Jack's lead, Dax did the same for him.

Jack lovingly nudged Dax to lie back, and when he did, he slid his pants down to his ankles. He stopped only to untie and remove Dax's sneakers, and then slipped Dax's pants over his feet. He pulled off both socks and threw them, along with Dax's pants, to the corner of the cabin. Dax watched with anticipation as Jack slowly unzipped his khaki pants and shimmied them down his muscular legs until they puddled around his ankles. Jack knelt between Dax's legs, and all he could think about was Dax, his hot, muscular body waiting to be taken. He began to nibble at Dax's stiffening cock through his underwear. Still not used to this unfamiliar territory, he tried to remember what had felt the best when done to him in his limited experiences. He turned his head to the side and lightly ran his teeth up and down the shaft of Dax's cock, teasing and tormenting with every stroke.

Dax began to slowly raise and lower his hips, responding to Jack's tender touch. Jack pulled the waistband of Dax's underwear down far enough to expose his thick, rock-hard cock. In one slow, tantalizing move, Jack took the head of Dax's cock into his mouth and slid down as far as he could go without gagging. He inhaled the sweet smell of Dax's manhood through his crotch hairs, stopped, and slowly slid his mouth back up again. He found a comfortable rhythm and began to move in slow, even strokes as Dax moaned with pleasure.

He reluctantly released him when Dax took him by his upper arms and pulled Jack to him. Dax plunged his tongue into Jack's mouth and consumed him with every ounce of passion he could muster. Jack gave way to the assault as he massaged Dax's massive chest. He broke the kiss and started again working his way down Dax's washboard abs to what he'd sampled minutes ago. When he reached Dax's erect cock, he again took it into his mouth and caressed it gently.

"I need to be inside you so badly," Jack whispered.

Dax didn't respond. The silence was deafening.

Jack thought, *Damn, I shouldn't have asked him to do that again. He said he was the one who was usually the aggressor.*

"I want that too," Dax said.

"No pressure," Jack said.

"I know," Dax said as he smiled up at Jack.

Jack had been prepared this time. He'd placed the condoms and lube near the bed, and now reached over and grabbed them and laid them on the bed. He slowly repositioned Dax's legs, placing Dax's feet against his chest. Softly, he kissed Dax's toes. He lubricated his fingers and slowly approached his hole and began to massage his pucker.

Dax tensed as he felt Jack's finger touch him. He took a deep breath and tried relaxed his inner muscles as Jack gently probed his hole with his finger. Jack took his time, caringly massaging and probing to get Dax used to the feeling and to make sure he was relaxed enough to accept him.

"Are you ready?" Jack asked.

"Yes," flowed eagerly from Dax's mouth.

Slowly, Jack positioned his dick against Dax and pushed into him. Dax gasped when he felt Jack's girth. Jack was still for a few minutes, to allow Dax to adjust to the invasion. Slowly, Jack started moving until his dick disappeared into Dax's accepting asshole. Dax swallowed hard and took deep breaths as the pain turned to pleasure, and he relaxed into the ride. When Jack saw the shift take place, he began to move in and out of Dax, increasing the pace as he went.

"You feel so good," Jack whispered.

Dax's cock seemed to get harder every time Jack thrust fully into him. Dax took both of his legs and wrapped them around Jack's torso. With this maneuver, Jack moved his body closer to Dax's, and he felt his cock penetrating deeper into him. Through hot breath, Jack drove his tongue into Dax's mouth. Dax closed his eyes, and Jack couldn't believe how much he yearned for this man.

Jack spread some lube on Dax's dick and began to slide his hand up and down over the head, down the shaft, to the base, and back up again. Dax was so hard, Jack feared he would burst with pleasure any minute. Jack felt his balls begin to tighten and knew he was about to cum. He started to pick up speed and willed his hand to match his pace, stroke for stroke, as he jerked Dax off.

Within seconds, Jack and Dax simultaneously shot their loads: Dax over his washboard stomach, onto his large, cut chest, and finally stopping at his chin, Jack filling Dax's warm, inviting ass. Out of breath, and exhausted from the intense lovemaking, Jack collapsed on top of Dax, and they lay there in silence.

They had just gone to a place never imagined, and there was no reason to believe that they would ever turn back. Jack finally broke the silence.

"Dax?"

"Yeah, Captain."

"I think that was the best sex I've ever had."

"Ya think?" Dax asked.

"Let me rephrase that, I know that was the best sex I've ever had."

"That's better," Dax said, as he shifted a little under Jack and deposited him at his side. Jack relaxed his head on Dax's chest as Dax wrapped his arm around him and held him tightly. Jack gently caressed Dax's chest and teased his nipples.

Eventually, they hit the head and cleaned up before they climbed back into bed. They lay there spooning, with Dax's back tucked against Jack's chest and Jack's protective arms surrounding him, where Dax thought he could stay forever.

EVERYONE was awakened by beating on their doors and Dona yelling, "Rise and shine, you sleepyheads. It's going to be a great day!"

"I guess her hangover is all better," Dax said as he nuzzled his head into Jack's neck. "I don't want to get up, Jack. Make her stop."

Jack looked at the clock and saw it was 4:35. He looked out the porthole, and the sun was just starting to rise. According to last night's weather report, the high for the day was going to be about sixty-eight, but he was very sure it was much colder than that right now.

He lay back down and snuggled in against Dax's back and pushed as close as he could get. "We need to get her a girlfriend," Jack whispered. "That might keep her in bed a little later."

"Don't count on it. When we're working, she's relentless," Dax confessed.

They heard banging again on the door. "I hear you talking so I know you're up. Don't make me come in there."

"You wouldn't dare!" Jack yelled.

The door instantly flew open, and Dona leaped into the bed and said, "Oh, I wouldn't, huh?"

Dax started laughing and yelled, "Get out, you pushy lesbian!"

"Who are you calling pushy?" she asked as she rolled on top of Dax and tried to wiggle in between him and Jack.

"Come on, boys, get up," she whined. "We've got a lot to do before the first dive, and I'm starving."

"Then go start breakfast, and I'll be out to help you in a second," Dax pleaded.

"No need," Mac said as he poked his head into the little cabin. "I'm on it."

"Oh great," Jack chimed in. "You might as well join the party."

"No thanks, I'll pass, but thanks for the offer." Just then, Brad joined him at the door and peered in at the sight of the three of them in bed.

"Kinky," he said. "Jack, you never cease to amaze me."

"Get out!" Jack yelled as he threw his pillow at the door.

"Okay, okay, we're going," Mac said as he dragged Brad by the hand in the direction of the galley.

Dona got out of the bed and said, "Seriously, you guys, we have a lot to do. Get up, please."

"I know one thing," Jack said. "From now on, we never, ever go to bed without locking our door."

"Amen to that," Dax said.

"You just go right ahead and do that," Dona said as she stormed out of the door and slammed it behind her.

"Is she always this cheerful in the morning?" Jack asked.

"Nope, sometimes she's very grumpy," Dax said as he swung his legs over the side of the bed and ran his fingers through his hair. He forced himself to stand. "I'll grab a quick shower, you want to join me?" he asked.

"The short answer is yes," Jack said. "But haven't we been over this? The two of us can't fit in my shower."

"Yeah, I guess you're right," Dax said. "But you can't blame a guy for trying."

Jack looked at Dax with a loving expression. "I hope you never stop trying."

"I won't," Dax said, and he added a wink. "See you in a few."

Jack laid his head back down on the pillow, raised his hands, and linked his fingers behind his head. He crossed his ankles under the sheet and looked up at the ceiling. Suddenly, he had this urge to smile. He mused about how his life had changed since he'd met Dax. From dull, boring, and lonely to hot, happy, and exciting, all in less than a month. His life finally had meaning, and he had someone to care for and protect. In that very moment he knew that this was what he'd been waiting for all of his life. "Thank you, Dax," he whispered.

AS JACK waited for his turn to shower, he went over the game plan in his head. For the next couple of days, Dax and Dona would be diving alone. The first day they would identify and mark the hull where the explosives were to be attached, and the next day they would secure the explosives on the previously marked locations and ready them for detonation.

Still thinking about the mission, Jack rolled over onto his side and faced the head door, waiting for his next glimpse of Dax. He really wanted to make the dives with Dax, but he knew that Dax and Dona had done this drill so many times that they would be quicker and more thorough working together. In addition, Jack had recalled Dax saying that they had to follow the ship's plans very closely, because if they accidentally placed an explosive on one of the main structural supports, and that compartment wasn't already flooded, the combination of the explosives and the underwater pressure could collapse the hull, leaving that portion of the interior permanently inaccessible.

Dona had warned them that they would be using more powerful underwater explosives this go-round, and that safety was of the utmost importance. She explained that once the explosives were set, she and Dax would surface and the *Lindsey C* would be moved to a safe distance. The explosives would then be detonated from the surface using electronic detonation technology, or EDT. They would blow enough holes along both sides of the hull for clear access and maneuverability, but the most difficult and dangerous part of the expedition would be to navigate within the bowels of the ship. They had all reviewed the ship's plans and realized that the commercial ship interiors built during that time period were quite small, and navigating that environment with their cumbersome diving gear would be difficult at best, very slow going and extremely dangerous, and everyone had to be on their game.

Just then, Dax opened the door and popped out of the head with just a towel thrown over his shoulder.

"Come here, and let me dry your back," Jack said.

"Oh, no, Captain. If I get anywhere near that bed, I'm going to leave this cabin deflowered yet again, and I have my reputation to consider."

"What reputation?" Jack asked.

"Very funny!" Dax shouted over his shoulder as he wrapped his towel around his waist and opened the cabin door.

"Damn, I was *this* close," Jack said as he held up his thumb and forefinger with a small space between them. "You won't get away so easy next time!" he shouted as he got up and headed for the shower.

IN TWENTY minutes the *Lindsey C* came to life, as everyone was on deck and quite busy. Dax and Dona again studied the plans of the ship, Mac and Brad checked and rechecked the dive equipment, and from the bridge, Jack used radar to continue the reconnaissance of any ships passing within a three-mile radius. Once the bleep appeared on his screen, he would use the binoculars to locate and identify the ship for later research. Currently, no ships had passed twice, and no vessel was anchored within a two-mile radius. So far, all seemed clear.

By mid-day, Dax and Dona were suiting up for the first dive. They knew they would have to make several dives because of the water temperature, but their goal was to get the entire hull marked before sunset. When Dax and Dona were ready to enter the water, Brad helped Dona on with her equipment, and she jumped in with a set of waterproof ship's plans and a large, white wax marker. Dax had a crowbar in one hand and his mask in the other. He would use the crowbar to help clean the hull, so Dona could get a good adhesion when they attached the explosives and adequately mark the spot as well. He stood still on the swim platform while Jack helped get his tanks on and secured. When he was suited up and about to enter the water, Jack put both hands on the outside of Dax's shoulders and whispered, "I just found you, and I'm not ready to give you up, so be careful."

Dax smiled, "You can't get rid of me that easy, Captain."

Jack turned to Dona floating nearby. "Dona, you guys be careful, and take care of him for me. I'll have the communication equipment on, and we'll stay in touch the entire time."

Dona nodded, and Jack stole a kiss right before Dax slipped on his mask. Dax jumped in feet first, holding his face mask, and kicked his way over to Dona. He gave Jack the okay sign, and they both raised the air hose on their BC and slowly descended.

Jack checked the radio receiver, "Radio check, Dax, do you read me?"

"Loud and clear, Captain. Visibility is about thirty feet, and the currents are mild. It should be a great dive."

"Be… careful…."

"Will do, Jack," Dax responded.

"Jeez, you two," Dona whined. "It's not like we're going down to the *Titanic* or something. Give me a break."

"You're just jealous that no one's on the surface patiently waiting for your return," Jack laughed.

"Maybe I am, and maybe I'm not, but I can guarantee you that if I did have someone waiting for me up there, we wouldn't be carrying on like you two ladies," she screeched through her mask.

Jack conceded. "Okay, okay. Have a safe dive, both of you!"

DAX and Dona quickly fell into a familiar routine. Dona read the ship's plans as they made their way along the hull. According to the plans, she stopped at each pre-identified location and Dax used the crowbar to clear away a small area of the one-hundred-plus years of barnacles and underwater growth. When the hull was as clean as he could get it, he marked the spot with the wax marker and moved on to the next location. The going was slow but steady, and he and Jack made small talk along the way, which helped pass the time. They'd just finished the port side when Dax's underwater alarm indicated that he was getting low on oxygen.

"How's your oxygen, sis?" Dax asked.

"About gone. Yours?" she responded.

"Same," he said. "This is a good stopping point. What do you say we surface, exchange our tanks, and get back down here and get the starboard side marked?"

"Okay by me," Dona said.

Jack chimed in. "Hey, guys, we'll meet you on the swim platform. See you in a few."

"Okay, baby," Dax responded.

Dax turned in the direction of the *Lindsey C* and caught movement out of the corner of his eye. "Dona, did you pick up any motion over there near the reef?" he asked as he pointed over his right shoulder.

She quickly looked in that direction and scanned the reef system. "No. Why?"

"I don't know," he said. "I think I caught some movement a second ago."

"You want to go check it out?" she asked.

"Nah, it was probably nothing."

"Jack, you still there?" Dax asked. "Did you copy that?"

"I'm here, and yes, I copied," he replied.

"Any activity on the surface?"

"Mac and Brad have been on the lookout since your descent, and there's nothing out of the ordinary to report."

"I guess it was nothing. See you in a couple minutes, baby."

"I can hardly wait," Jack responded.

Dona piped up. "Oh jeez, here we go again."

They all laughed as Dona and Dax started swimming to the boat.

THEIR observer finally gasped for air when he saw the two divers swimming in the opposite direction. Not wanting to create any air bubbles, he was almost blue from holding his breath. At one point, he felt certain that one of them had picked up on his movement, and his cover had been blown. He thought they were about to swim over and check it out, so he had bolted for cover. He'd hidden beyond the reef, froze, and held his breath. With the immediate danger now gone, he swam along the reef line, watching the two divers swim away. When they were no longer in sight, he moved over to the wreck and checked out their handiwork. He'd been watching them for ten minutes, and he saw that they were clearing the hull and marking certain locations. He was now sure they were marking locations for explosives. They appeared to have the port side finished, which meant they would be back soon to finish the starboard. He quickly moved away and swam off into the distance.

DAX and Dona surfaced within minutes and, as promised, Mac and Brad were there to help them aboard. Dona was first on deck. She released her BC, and Mac slid the BC and tanks off of her back. When Jack reached the deck, he was already yelling, "Welcome back! How was it down there?"

Dax was climbing out of the water, and Jack almost pushed Brad overboard trying to get to him.

"Look out, you crazy new homosexual," Brad said as he sidestepped Jack's flailing arms. "You almost pushed me overboard."

"That'll teach you to get between a new homosexual and his boyfriend," Jack hissed.

Brad smiled and turned to ascend the stairs to the deck. Without really thinking, he lifted his leg and used his foot to push Jack overboard. Jack hit the water with a very ungraceful splash, and when he surfaced with a shocked and angry look on his face, he was blood-red.

"Bradford, I'll get you for that!" he yelled as he swam back to the swim platform. Everyone was laughing hysterically, including Dax, as Jack climbed up the swim ladder. Many years of being on the water, and the sheer fact that he was pretty damn clumsy, had taught Jack never to carry anything valuable in his pockets while on board, so nothing was lost or ruined, except his pride.

When he climbed the ladder to the platform, Jack looked at Dax, who was still bent over, laughing uncontrollably. Jack crossed his arms over his chest and looked at Dax with a hurt look. "You too?" he asked. "I expected them to enjoy this, but you?"

"I'm really sorry, Jack," Dax said with an apologetic look as he straightened up. "I really can't help myself. You don't know this about me, but I lose it when people fall. Whether it's off of a boat or bicycle or if they stumble or trip, it doesn't really matter how they fall—if they fall, I can't control myself. I get so tickled that I can't stop laughing." He looked at Dona with a sympathetic look. "Come on, sis. Help me out here, will you?" Dax pleaded.

Dona looked at Jack. "It's true, Jack," she said. "I can vouch for him. I once saw him get kicked off a city bus when we were kids because an old lady tripped and fell down the steps while she was getting off at her stop. Dax laughed so hard the bus driver gave him his money back, put him off of the bus, and told him to never ride his bus again."

Jack had a questioning look on his face, which slowly turned into a smile. "Fine, but for the record, I didn't fall. I was pushed," he said as he glanced in Brad's direction. "Furthermore, I'll let you have this one, but the next time, you're coming in after me."

"We'll see about that," Dax said as he pecked Jack on the lips. "You better get into some dry clothes while we change our tanks."

While Dax and Dona warmed in the sunshine, rehydrated, and had a quick snack, Mac and Brad retrieved new tanks from the dozen or so lined up in the tank storage compartment on the port side of the vessel. They disconnected the empty tanks from the regulators and removed the tanks from the BC's. They immediately carried the empty tanks to the empty tank storage compartment on the starboard side of the vessel and secured them in place. They then connected the regulators to the new tanks, opened the air valves, and tested the airflow. Everything seemed to be in good working condition. Dax and Dona were again ready to go.

Jack returned to the deck wearing dry clothes, and Dax met him halfway.

"Jack, I'm sorry I laughed at you. But in all honesty, you have to admit, it was pretty funny."

Jack started to grin, just a little, then he glanced over at Brad. Brad flashed a quick smile and said, "Am I forgiven?"

"You get a one-time pass, my friend," he replied. "The next time, you die a horrible death."

"We'll see about that," Brad said under his breath.

"What was that?" Jack asked.

"I said okay, I'm sorry," Brad stuttered.

"I thought that's what you said," Jack responded.

Dax and Dona suited up again, and within minutes they were under the surface. Jack checked the receivers again to make sure they had radio contact and resumed his scanning of the nearby vessels. As he scanned the horizon, he saw a large vessel newly anchored about a mile and a half from them. The bow was facing the *Lindsey C*, so he couldn't see the name or the hail port. *That boat wasn't there earlier, so it must have anchored recently*, he thought. *Dax thought he saw something earlier, so I'd better check it out.*

Jack radioed Dax and Dona and explained the situation, told them he was going to check it out, and asked them to keep an extra sharp eye out. Jack told them he would radio when he returned, and it was Dax's turn to be worried. "Be careful, Jack," he said.

He went down to the deck and filled Brad and Mac in as well. He turned the reconnaissance over to them and started the process of launching the twelve-foot tender with the outboard motor. The dinghy was stored on the bow and utilized the same winch system they had used to lower and raise the submersible. He attached the support straps to the winch and lowered the dinghy over the side.

He didn't make a beeline to the vessel, as he didn't want to attract any unwanted attention, so he went in the opposite direction and made a large circle around the vessel until he could get a clear view of the stern. It was difficult trying to focus the binoculars on the bouncing surf, but he finally managed it. He recognized the name right away, "прогулочный катер." *I'll be damned! What are you Russkies up to?*

He didn't want to head right back to the *Lindsey C* for the same reason he didn't head right to the ship in question, so he kept the little boat moving while he continued his loop. After about thirty minutes of bouncing around, he pulled up along the port side of the *Lindsey C*, away from the eyes of the other boat. He decided to leave the dinghy in the water, just in case. He didn't know what *just in case* might mean, but he was following his instincts and felt better knowing they had a quick escape.

Jack signaled for Brad and Mac to follow him up to the bridge while he radioed Dax and Dona. "All is fine here, how close are you to being done?" Jack asked.

"We're marking our last location and will surface in about ten minutes," Dax said. "How'd your mission go?"

"Roger that," Jack responded. "Good, I'll fill you in when you surface."

He told Mac and Brad about the Russian ship.

"Why didn't you tell Dax and Dona?" Mac asked.

"I'm not sure our radio frequencies aren't being monitored, and if they are, I didn't want anyone to know we're on to them. Besides, all we really know at this point is that a Russian ship has cruised by here, God only knows how many times, and is now anchored a little over a mile away."

Dax and Dona surfaced right on time, and all three men were there to meet them.

Dax and Dona looked at the expressions on their faces and back at each other. "What's happened?" Dax asked.

"You guys get unsuited and dry, and we'll meet in the salon in ten."

In just under ten minutes, everyone gave Jack their undivided attention as he explained his excursion and what he'd discovered. He also explained why he hadn't told them over the radio, and they both nodded with understanding.

"The more I think about it, the more certain I feel that I saw something or someone along the reef line during our earlier dive," Dax said. "I wanted to talk to you about it when we surfaced, but with all the commotion and Jack 'in the drink' and all, it just slipped my mind."

"Give us every detail you can remember," Jack said.

"We were about to surface, and over my right shoulder, some movement caught my eye. I instinctively glanced in that direction, but saw nothing. I brushed it off as a fish or something, but it really didn't sit right with me. The more I think about it, to catch my attention as it did, it was probably too big to be a fish."

"Could it have been a diver?" Jack asked. "I think it's perfectly reasonable to assume that a good diver could swim a mile or so underwater with no problems. Do you agree, Dax?"

"Without a doubt," Dax said.

They all sat in silence for a moment.

Dona was the one to speak first. "So," she said. "If someone is watching us and they know anything about salvage, they probably have a pretty good idea about our plan of attack. They watched us clean and mark the hull. I'm sure they know that the explosives come next. What if they're sitting back, allowing us to do the work, and once we find the gold, they plan on claiming it?"

"Wait!" Dax said. "For starters, we have no real proof that we're being watched. And if it turns out that we *are* being watched, we really don't know what they are watching us for, so let's not get ahead of ourselves."

Jack caught Dax's gaze and searched for some reassurance. Was he just saying that to make Dona feel better or did he really believe it? He wasn't sure, but Jack thought he saw a hell of a lot of worry hiding just beyond those gorgeous hazel eyes. He decided it was time to speak up. "I agree with Dax," he said. "Let's not jump to conclusions. Tomorrow we tighten up our operation and go about our business as planned. The only difference is that we keep a very close eye out for any strange activity."

Mac whistled and looked at Brad. "Well, Bradford, we wanted a little adventure and we certainly got it."

"This is so, James Bond," Brad replied.

"If you two want to call it quits, we'll certainly understand," Dona said. "We realize this is not what you bargained for."

Brad and Mac looked at each other. "No way," they said simultaneously. "We're in for the long haul," Mac said.

"Yeah, this is really cool," Brad added.

Dona smiled. "Okay then, it appears that we're all in," she concluded.

"Jack," Dax said. "What about you? You and the guys have the most to lose. It's your boat, and you and Brad and Mac have invested all the capital up front. No one would blame you if you decided to abort this expedition."

"Not on your life," Jack responded. "I'm here because I want to be. Sure, I love my boat, and it's no secret that I did this for the money, but I love you more. I got *you* out of this deal, and I'm not going to allow anything to happen to you. The only way I bolt is if you bolt, and I know that's not going to happen."

Brad and Mac looked at each other and smiled. Dona reached over and squeezed Dax's hand with a show of support. Jack rose from his seat and walked over and stood in front of Dax. He took Dax's two hands in his and pulled him to his feet. He watched Dax's face as the stress melted away and was replaced with the warmest smile he'd ever received.

"Thank you, Captain," Dax whispered warmly.

Jack simply nodded and pulled him in for a tight hug. Jack broke the embrace. "Now, what's the game plan?" he asked.

"Okay. Jack, if you don't mind, I think you should make tomorrow's dive with Dona and me."

"*Yes*," Jack said under his breath.

Dax smiled. "What did you say, Jack?"

"I meant *sure*," he said. "I'll dive with you tomorrow."

Dax continued. "That way we can move a lot faster, not having to watch our backs. Mac and Brad, do you guys feel comfortable standing guard on the surface? Can either of you handle a gun?"

Brad cleared his throat. "Excuse me! We's might be queers, but we's mountain queers," he said in his best hillbilly accent.

"Oh right, enough said," Dax chuckled. "Oh, one more thing. We're not sure if our communications are being monitored, so we better keep it short and to the point. Maybe a little normal bantering here and there to not let on that we suspect that we are being monitored, but nothing important unless it's absolutely necessary. Agreed?"

Everyone nodded.

"Then I guess we're as ready as we'll ever be. Tomorrow's going to be a very interesting day and we all need to be on our toes."

"I need a drink," Dona exclaimed. "Can I interest anyone else?"

"Hell yeah," Brad replied.

"Me too," Mac said.

Dona disappeared into her cabin and came out waving a very dusty bottle of red wine.

"I was saving this until we brought the gold on board," she said as she reached for the wine cork. "But now is as good a time as any."

"I'm in," Jack said, and Dax quickly followed suit.

Dona proudly showed everyone the label as she uncorked a 1965 vintage Cousino-Macul Antiguas Reservas Cabernet Sauvignon she'd bought in Italy several years back.

"I originally bought this to celebrate the find of the *Sarah Maria*," she explained. "And we all know what happened during that expedition."

Embarrassed again, Dax looked down at the floor.

"But," Dona continued, "if it hadn't been for that disaster, we wouldn't be here with you guys, and Dax wouldn't have found Jack."

"Amen to that," Jack said.

Dona looked over at Jack. "Can I assume that we don't have cheesecloth or a wine decanter on this tub?" she asked.

"Very funny," Jack said as he started rummaging through cabinets and drawers. "Will these do?" he asked as he held up an iced tea pitcher and a coffee filter.

Everyone laughed and Dona said, "I guess they'll have to."

She placed the coffee filter over the opening of the pitcher and carefully emptied the entire bottle of wine into the makeshift decanter.

While she allowed the wine to breathe, she gathered five glasses of various shapes and sizes and handed everyone one. After the appropriate breathing time, she evenly poured the wine into the awaiting glasses and held up hers in a toast. "To a safe and successful expedition," she said.

"Hear, hear," everyone responded.

They enjoyed the vintage bottle of wine as they discussed a number of topics, everyone trying really hard to keep the mood light and stay away from the worries of tomorrow's mission.

When everyone had finished drinking their wine, Dax collected the glasses and washed, dried, and put them away. He folded the towel and placed it over the edge of the sink. "I'm beat," he said. "We have a really long day tomorrow, so I think I'll turn in."

"Me too," Jack said with a wink.

"Imagine that," Brad whispered to Mac and Dona. They all laughed, including Jack, as he took Dax into his arms and kissed his cheek for everyone to see.

"Look at you with your public display of affection," Mac said. "You've really come a long way in a short time."

Jack smiled and winked over his shoulder as he led Dax to his stateroom for the evening.

"I guess that leaves the three of us," Brad said. "How about a game or two of Texas hold 'em?"

"Correction," Dona said. "That leaves the two of you, because I'm turning in too. I want to get a full night's sleep and be bright-eyed and bushy-tailed for tomorrow's activities."

"Party pooper," Brad said. "But you're right, I'm just blowing smoke. I'm really tired as well. You ready to turn in, Mac?" Mac nodded, and they turned off all but of one of the lights in the little salon and made sure the companionway door was locked before they retired.

Dona was putting the night-vision binoculars on her bedside table when she heard gentle footsteps and the closing of Mac and Brad's cabin door. She'd been watching the Russian ship for any activity for the last few minutes, but all looked very still. She crawled into her bunk and pulled the covers up to her neck. She lay there as she listened to muffled voices coming from their cabin, and she had no doubt they were discussing the same thing she'd been watching. She felt a sudden tinge of jealousy that they all had someone with which to discuss the latest developments, but quickly shook it off as she reminded herself that it was her decision to be single.

Chapter *11*

THE next morning, everyone was up at first light and moving around with a cautious attitude. Breakfast was cooked and served in record time, and seconds after the last breakfast dish was put away, the entire crew was on deck and ready to get the day started.

Dax and Dona were putting their dive suits on while Mac and Brad casually kept an eye on the Russian vessel, still anchored a little over a mile away. Jack appeared on deck with a speargun over his shoulder and a leather holster in his hand. He placed his gun on the table in front of Mac, and they exchanged knowing looks. He looked around and saw the surprised looks on everyone's faces, but to his amazement, no one raised a hand to object.

While Jack was getting his suit on, Dax—eager to get started—was the first to climb down to the swim platform. Brad carefully lowered the two cases of explosives and three weighted BC's with tanks and dive masks down the short set of stairs to Dax's outreached arms. Dax sat on the end of the swim platform with his feet hanging over the stern and put on his fins. Brad climbed down and slid the BC and tanks up behind him, and Dax slipped his arms into the BC and secured it down the front and around his waist. Dax twisted his body off of the platform and into the water in one quick move, and bobbed as he held onto the back of the boat. Dona climbed down and did the same, but before Jack descended the stairs, he put both hands on Mac's shoulders. He looked at the gun and back at Mac, and they both nodded.

"You have what you need, brother, and you have the bridge," he instructed. "If anything happens, do what you need to do. I trust you, man."

Jack gave Mac a hug and climbed down to the swim platform. All three of them were now in the chilly Alaskan waters and tapping their heads to give the "okay" signal. Brad gently lowered one case of explosives to Dax and one to Dona, and they descended one by one.

Mac took the gun from the table and headed for the bridge while Brad positioned himself midship, where he could keep a look out on their Russian friends.

When Mac reached the bridge, he flipped on the radio.

"Bridge to Jack," he said into the small handset.

"Read you loud and clear, Mac," Jack responded.

"Dax, do you read?" Mac asked.

"Roger that," Dax responded.

"Dona, how about you?" Mac repeated.

"Loud and clear, Mac," she responded.

"Okay, everyone," Dax said. "Let's get to work."

Jack adjusted his BC and hovered just above Dax and Dona with his speargun in his arms and a three-hundred-and-sixty-degree view of the wreck site. He watched and admired from above as Dax and Dona performed like a well-oiled machine, their years of working together very evident in their skilled movements. Before Jack knew it, forty-five minutes had passed.

"How's it coming down there, Dax?" Jack asked.

"Pretty good, we're right on schedule. We're just finishing the port side and about to move over to the starboard," Dax responded. "How's it looking up there?"

"Clear as a bell," Jack said. "No sign of sharks, if that's what you mean."

"Perfect. Hey, guys," Dax said. "To be safe, let's go ahead and switch over to tank number two."

"Roger that," Dona and Jack replied. "Switching to tank number two."

Jack continued his lookout while Dax and Dona diligently worked to secure the remaining explosives to the starboard side of the wreck. In just under an hour, Dax was alerting Jack that they were on the last explosive and would need about twenty minutes more to arm each electronic explosive before they could surface.

Exactly twenty minutes later, Jack glanced down at the wreck and saw two rows of flashing green lights. Dax and Dona were looking up at him, and Dax gave the thumbs up sign.

"Ready when you are, Captain," Dax said.

"I'm right behind you guys," Jack replied. "We're on our way, Mac."

"We'll be ready," Mac responded.

Brad was just getting down to the swim platform when Dax and Dona surfaced about ten feet from the stern. Another thirty seconds and Jack was right behind them.

Dax floated the empty explosive containers to Brad and then slipped out of his BC. Brad handed the containers to Mac one by one and then took Dax's BC and lifted it out of the water and placed it on the swim platform. Dona and Jack did the same, and just before Jack climbed onto the boat, he carefully handed the loaded speargun to Brad, which Brad then slowly handed to Mac. They were all on board, congratulating each other on a successful dive.

"Well, this is it, boys," Dona said. "We're almost there."

Brad was so excited he could hardly contain himself. "When do we detonate?" he asked.

"Shortly," Dax said. "Once we get some dry clothes on, we'll pick up the anchor and move the *Lindsey C* to a safe distance, and we're ready to go."

"Brad, any activity topside while we were away?" Jack asked.

"Just a couple of cruise ships coming and going," Brad responded.

"How about our friends over there?" Jack said as he gestured to the Russian vessel.

"Nothing," Mac said. "It's almost like they know we're watching them."

"Interesting," Dax said.

"Dax, maybe you were right," Dona admitted. "It's possible that I was just being really paranoid."

"Time will tell," Dax said. "But if we're gonna have company, I would imagine that it would be right after we blow the hull. Let's get some dry clothes on and get this show on the road."

"Not so fast, guys," Brad added. "Jack, I did notice one of those fishing boats you scratched off your surveillance. I think you said you knew the captain."

"Which one?" Jack asked.

"The *Jolly Roger*," Brad replied.

"Roger Hillstrom owns and operates that boat," Jack recalled. "We have a few beers every now and then. I don't know him that well, but I don't think he would be involved in any funny business."

"What do you define as 'funny business'?" Brad asked.

"What do *you* consider funny business?" Jack asked.

"The *Jolly Roger* passed four times in the last two hours," Brad said.

"That's odd," Jack said. "Which direction did you first see him heading?"

"He was heading out to sea the first time," Brad explained.

"That's pretty odd," Jack admitted. "If he had engine trouble, he may have had to return to port, but he wouldn't have enough time to reach port and make it back here in two hours."

"Which means that he didn't go all the way back to port before he turned around," Mac said.

"You're right," Jack conceded. "But he could have hit one of the smaller ports along the canal instead of going all the way back to Skagway. But...." Jack held up a finger. "It usually takes a hell of a lot longer than a couple of hours to get a mechanic to any dock to diagnose and repair a problem. All we can do is keep an eye on him," Jack said.

"One more thing," Brad added. "On the third and fourth passes, he swung very wide, as if to avoid being seen by us."

"Now that's even more interesting," Dax said.

"Still think I'm being paranoid, boys?" Dona asked as she passed them on the way to her cabin to change.

The four men all exchanged looks, no one wanting to say any more. Dax and Jack followed Dona and went down below to change into dry clothes, while Mac and Brad continued their surveillance of the Russian vessel and scanned for the *Jolly Roger* or any suspicious new visitors.

Twenty minutes later, Jack was on the bridge of the *Lindsey C*, with both engines purring like kittens. Mac and Brad were on the bow at the anchor controls, awaiting the signal to raise the anchor. Jack put the engines in gear as he gave Mac the signal to start the anchor winch. The boat started slowly inching forward in time with the anchor winch as it started retrieving the anchor from the canal floor.

Dax and Dona joined Jack on the bridge, carrying a metal briefcase containing the minicomputer used to electronically detonate the explosives. Dax opened the case and booted up the computer as Jack inched his way forward. When the computer was booted, Dax ran a check to make sure all the explosives were identified, armed, and ready for detonation.

With the anchor on board and secure, Jack headed for his anticipated position. About a quarter-mile upstream from the wreck site, he picked up the radio to do a security call.

"Security – Security – Security. This is the seventy-five-foot, dive charter vessel *Lindsey C* idling in the Lynn Canal approximately one-quarter mile north of latitude 58.9748 and longitude -135.227. We are conducting approved salvaging exercises utilizing underwater explosives at the previously mentioned position and advise all vessels to avoid this position for the next sixty minutes. I am standing by on channel one six for any concerned vessels. *Lindsey C* out."

"Hey, Dax, sixty minutes should give us enough time to detonate all the explosives and get back into position over the wreck site, right?" Jack asked.

"I think so," Dax responded. "That is, unless we have any explosives that malfunction and don't detonate."

"What are the odds of that happening?" Jack asked.

"Pretty unlikely, but certainly possible," Dax said.

"How will you know if one doesn't detonate?" Jack asked.

"We detonate the explosives one at a time to make sure we don't miss one and leave a live explosive beneath the surface," Dax explained.

"Oh, got it," Jack said. "If we have any malfunctions, I'll just do another security call."

Within minutes, the system chimed, and all the lights flashed green, meaning a connection had been established with each explosive, and they were ready to go.

"Here goes nothing," Dax said as he pushed the first button.

They felt a small vibration underfoot and looked to the site, where a large air bubble surfaced, spraying water about ten feet into the air.

"Yes!" Jack yelled.

Over the next thirty minutes, Dax detonated all the remaining explosives, one by one, counting and watching the effects until all the explosives were successfully detonated.

Brad and Mac were on the bow, jumping up and down and pumping their fists in the air like kids on Christmas morning, while Jack simply smiled like a kid in a candy store. When it appeared that the last of the explosives had detonated, Jack asked, "We're good?"

"We're good," Dax replied.

Jack again picked up the radio.

"Security – Security – Security. This is the seventy-five-foot, dive charter vessel *Lindsey C* idling in the Lynn Canal approximately one-quarter mile north of latitude 58.9748 and longitude -135.227. We have completed our approved salvaging exercises utilizing underwater explosives at the previously mentioned position, and the waterway is once again open to all traffic in either direction. I am standing by on channel one six for any concerned vessels. *Lindsey C* out."

Jack put the engines in gear, and the *Lindsey C* slowly moved toward her next destination. When they reached the correct position, just short of the wreck, Jack gave Mac and Brad the signal, and they released the winch and the anchor began its descent into the chilly waters. They all met on deck, and Dax and Dona began to suit up. Dax looked up and saw Jack wasn't putting his suit on. "Jack, are you going to suit up?" he asked.

"I think I'll pass on this dive," Jack said. "If our Russian friends are going to try anything, I think it would be pretty soon, and I want to be ready for them."

Dax opened his mouth to say something, but before he could speak, Jack yelled, "Hey, Bradford! Since I've already been down, why don't you and Mac make this dive, and I'll stay topside to keep an eye on things."

Brad looked up from helping Dona with her suit with a broad smile and said, "Really?"

Dax closed his mouth and glared at Jack with a look Jack couldn't identify. Maybe it was concern and maybe it was disappointment, but either way, Jack knew he was making the right decision.

"I don't like the idea of you being up here alone," Dax finally said in a frustrated tone.

"He won't be alone," Mac said as he squeezed Dax's shoulder. "I'll stay topside with him while Brad makes the dive."

Dax looked somewhat relieved and mouthed the words "thank you" to Mac.

"Mac," Brad said as he grabbed him around the waist. "I really want you to make the dive. I'll stay topside and protect Captain Jack from the mean, old pirates."

Jack let out a hearty laugh and Mac started to protest, but Brad held up his hand to stop him.

"Look, Mac," Brad continued. "You're a better diver than I am, and I'll have plenty of time to go down tomorrow. Besides, I feel more comfortable diving with you anyway."

Mac again tried to protest, but Brad wouldn't have any of it.

"Now get your happy butt suited up so you can go and find your husband some gold," Brad said.

Knowing he'd lost again, Mac conceded and suited up for the dive.

"Hey, Mac," Dax said. "How are you with a camera?"

"Fair to middling," Mac responded. "Why?"

"Do you think you can handle an underwater camera to document our dive?" Dax asked.

"Sure, I'll give it a shot."

"So here's the plan," Dax explained. "Dona will take the lead, I'll go in after her, and you can bring up the rear, filming the entire operation. If we find anything we can carry out safely, we'll do it. If not, we'll mark the spot and come in tomorrow with more salvage equipment."

"Sounds like a plan," Mac said.

"Dona," Dax asked, "you okay with that?"

"A-okay, Dax," she replied. "Can we get this show on the road?"

Jack handed each of them a high-beam underwater flashlight and, in addition, gave Mac the underwater camera and the speargun. Minutes later they were making their descent.

Jack and Brad did another radio check, then went up to the bridge to get a better view of the Russian vessel. When they reached the bridge, Jack slapped a forty-five in Brad's hand and said, "Don't be afraid to use it."

Brad checked the safety and ejected the magazine to make sure the gun was fully loaded. He snapped the magazine back into the handle with the palm of his hand and put the gun in the waistband of his jeans. After they did their radio check, Jack explained to Brad that he would keep a close eye on the Russian vessel, but based on the way the wind was blowing, if they sent divers into the water from the port side of the vessel, he wouldn't be able to see them. In addition, they had no idea how many people were on board the boat and how many were divers and how many were crew.

"I suggest we get our dive equipment ready just in case we have to go in after the guys," Brad suggested.

"Good idea," Jack said. "I'll keep an eye out here if you want to take care of the equipment."

"Will do," Brad responded. "I'll be back shortly," he said over his shoulder as he exited the bridge.

Jack lifted the handset to the radio, "Bridge to Dax," he said.

"I'm here, Jack."

"Is everything okay down there?" Jack asked.

"So far, so good," Dax replied. "The explosives seem to have done their job well. The hull is intact but open. I'll fill you in on the details when we surface."

"Roger that. Be careful, and keep an eye out for sharks," Jack urged.

"I've got their backs, Jack," Mac said.

"And we've got yours," Dona added.

"It sounds like a regular love fest down there," Jack said. "Bridge out."

WITH Mac filming their every move, Dax and Dona completed their inspection of the blown hull, trying to locate the best entry point. From the ship's plans, they knew that the cargo hold compartments ran midship to the engine room in the stern, and the living quarters, including the purser's office, were forward of the cargo hold compartments into the bow. They both agreed to enter the hull at the largest strategic opening, which was port side, just aft of midship.

Dona was going to be the first person to enter the *Anna Wyoming* in over one hundred years. One-hundred-and-twelve years to be exact, and Dax was right behind her, with Mac getting it all on film. At the entrance of the wreck, Dona stopped and braced herself on the hull of the ship. She took a deep breath in an attempt to slow down the adrenaline flow already reaching her veins and entered the dreary, dark, watery tomb. Her heart was racing with unbridled excitement, and she could sense her twin behind her experiencing the same feelings. Over the years, they had shared with one another what they felt each time they stepped back into another world, but even if they hadn't, she could sense his excitement, and she imagined that he could sense hers.

As they entered the ship, the interior of the hull was just as they had assumed it would be. Long, dark, narrow corridors ran bow to stern, with oval, watertight hatches every fifteen or so feet connecting the compartments. They knew that if emergency protocol had been followed, all the hatches should be securely closed. They also knew that midway through every other corridor was a hatch leading port to starboard, and those were the hatches that would lead them to the cargo holds.

The beams of their flashlights weren't strong enough to see any farther than fifteen feet or so, but they'd studied the plans so extensively that they didn't need any illumination to know where they were going. Moving her flashlight around as she went, Dona felt her way along the first corridor, heading toward the bow. She approached the first hatch connecting the narrow corridors.

They'd strategically placed the explosives along the hull to make sure that every compartment would be flooded, but they had no way of knowing if they had succeeded until they actually opened the hatch.

Dona braced herself against the hull for leverage and attempted to turn the wheel on the hatch.

The hatch opened into the next corridor, so if for any reason the cabin on the other side of the door had *not* been flooded, the vacuum pressure and the rush of water could be deadly, depending on the size of the compartment and how long it took to flood.

"Damn it, the wheel won't budge," Dona said as she struggled to get it to turn.

"Let me have a shot at it," Dax said. "I'll go up, you go down."

In order to change places in the tiny corridor, Dona floated herself to the floor and eased back in the direction from which she'd come while Dax hovered above and took her place.

Dax handed Dona his flashlight and removed a crowbar attached to his dive belt. He locked the crowbar into the opening of the round, valve-like handle and braced himself just as Dona had done. He used all his strength and leverage, and little by little the handle started to turn.

"Here we go—brace yourselves," Dax said. "It's opening."

Dona and Mac braced themselves as best they could as Dax forced the hatch to the next compartment to open. The wheel stopped turning, which meant it was completely open, but nothing happened. Dax slid his crowbar back into his dive belt as Dona handed him his flashlight. "Here goes nothing," he said as he gave the door a gentle push.

The door opened with surprisingly little effort, and a fish darted through the opening and ran right into Dax's mask.

Dax squealed. Dona laughed and said, "Sissy."

"It just surprised me," he replied in an angry tone.

"Uh-huh," she said.

He pushed the door open and peered inside. Again, Dona took the lead and swam past him, through the hatch and into the small corridor.

Suddenly she stopped. Dax heard her gasp for breath.

"Dona, what's wrong? Are you okay?" he asked.

"Oh my God, Dax, look," she said as she pointed to the floor of the corridor.

Dax looked down where Dona was hovering and a small gasp left his lips as well. Lying on the floor of the corridor, untouched for over a hundred years, were two perfectly intact skeletons, seemingly locked in an embrace.

"They must have known the end was near," Dax said. "But it appears that whatever happened to this ship must have happened pretty quickly, that these people didn't have a chance to get topside."

Dona moved her flashlight over the skeletons, but quickly stopped when something reflected off the beam of her flashlight. Still around the neck of one of the skeletons was a gold chain of some sort, with a medallion attached. On further investigation, the other skeleton was found to be wearing the same medallion. In addition, each left hand wore what appeared to be a gold band around their ring finger.

"Do you think they were married to each other?" she asked.

"We'll never know," Dax said.

Jack had heard the gasps from the surface and his voice quickly invaded their ears. "What's going on down there, guys?" he asked. "Are you okay?"

"We're fine, Jack, just a couple of skeletons. Not unexpected or the first time we've seen them, but they always seem to draw the same reaction from both of us every time we encounter them."

"Okay, just know your conversations are being monitored very closely," Jack said. "If you need anything, I'm here."

"We know, Jack, thanks!" They were aware that Jack's statement was a reminder that they might not be the only one hearing their conversation.

Dona and Dax moved very cautiously over the bones, trying their best not to disturb the couple's final resting place. Mac did the same, but paused overhead to get a quick shot in hopes that someday they might be identified by the medallions or rings.

Dona approached the second hatch and was able to open this one on her own. She opened it, and Dax took the lead this time.

He moved his flashlight in every direction; there were human remains strewn all about this corridor. Dax assumed that more remains were in this corridor because it had access to the cargo hold hatch, and people were probably trying to get topside.

"More remains," he said to himself as much as to Dona and Mac. "Be careful."

He felt certain that the hatch leading to the interior of the ship, and hopefully the cargo hold, would be just ahead on his right, but as he inched along slowly, he was amazed that after so many years, this corridor was much more pristine, compared to the last.

"So many remains," Dona said, looking around. "And it's so odd the way they're spread all around, compared to the way they were in the other corridor."

"From the looks of it, I'll bet this cabin wasn't flooded until we detonated the explosives," Dax said. "The force of the flooding must have disturbed the remains."

He suddenly felt very responsible for upsetting the final resting place of so many people. He bowed his head and said a silent prayer for the people who'd lost their lives so tragically, and then continued forward. He felt his way along the inside wall, looking for any signs of the hatch, but still nothing.

"Mac, are you getting all of this?" Dax asked.

"Everything," Mac responded.

Suddenly the door came into view, and it was, amazingly, right where it should have been.

"There it is," Dax said.

"I see it," Dona replied.

"Me too," Mac added.

Dax again braced himself and placed his hands on the wheel and attempted to turn it. Much to his surprise, it turned with no problem.

Then a thought occurred to him. He stopped turning and froze.

"What is it, Dax? Why did you stop?" Dona asked.

"What if the interior compartment is not flooded?" he said. "Mac, close the hatch behind us."

"What, are you crazy?" Mac asked, starting to feel a little claustrophobic. "We'll be locked in."

"No, seriously, close the hatch and secure it," Dax insisted.

"Why? What if we need to get out of here in a hurry?" he asked.

"It's just a hunch," Dax said. "But if it's not flooded, we might be able to protect whatever is in there from the onslaught of the water pressure."

"Okay, let's just say we close the hatch behind me and we open the cargo hatch and it's not flooded. How will we get out?" Mac asked.

"It'll be tricky," Dax said. "But if we close the cargo hatch behind us when we exit and then reopen the corridor hatch, the small corridor will again flood. It'll be crazy for a second until everything stabilizes, but it shouldn't be that bad."

Again they heard Jack's voice come over the radio, this time a little more frantic. "Don't take any unnecessary risks, Dax Powers," he said. "Let the damn cargo hold flood, and do your job."

"Jack, if the cargo hold is not flooded, we may have a chance to preserve whatever else is in there," Dax pleaded.

"You have no idea if there *is* anything else in there. Why risk your lives?" Jack asked.

"Okay, let's do it," Mac said.

"I'm in," Dona said.

"Damn it, Dax," Jack said. "If you don't die down there, you'll die up here when I get my hands on you."

"I know, Jack," Dax said. "I love you too."

Mac closed the hatch behind him and turned the wheel until it was tight. He swam over and joined Dax and Dona at the interior hatch.

Dax began to slowly turn the wheel again. Then he stopped once more. "Okay, once I release the lock, the pressure should force the hatch to open, and the water will rush from the corridor into the cargo hold until it levels out. Hold on, and try to remain on your feet. If all goes well, we'll be left standing in shin-deep water," he said.

Dax gave the wheel one last turn. The pressure forced the wheel of the hatch right out of his hands and within seconds the corridor was almost empty. "It's not flooded!" Dax yelled.

"Oh my God, we did it!" Mac added.

They were now standing in shin-deep water and suddenly feeling every pound of the weight from their dive equipment.

"We've got to make this quick," Dax said. "I'm sure there's no oxygen in the compartment, and we don't have a hell of a lot left in our tanks. If we find anything worth preserving, we'll close the hatch back up and make another dive. If we don't find anything but the gold, we can flood the compartment to make it easier for us to maneuver and salvage. The water certainly won't hurt the gold."

"Sounds like a plan," Dona said.

"Agreed," said Mac.

Chapter *12*

DAX waved his flashlight into the cargo hold and started looking around. He immediately spotted wooden crates stacked in the center of the compartment. *There's more gold here than we thought,* he said to himself. He quickly did an inventory on the number of crates in the hold, ten across, by ten deep, by five high. He did the math, *that's five hundred crates.*

Dona and Mac helped Dax awkwardly step through the small hatch from the corridor into the ankle-deep water of the cargo hold. Fighting his swim fins and the weight of his tanks, he slowly wobbled over to the stack of crates. He again used his crowbar to dig into the seal of one of the wooden crates. The crates were brittle and weak from age and it took him only seconds to pry one open. The anticipation was killing him, but when he finally lifted the lid, he found six perfectly preserved, one-gallon aluminum cans. He used his glove to wipe away whatever sediments had accumulated over the last hundred years and read the label: "Salted Fish."

"What the fuck?" he said out loud.

"What?" Dona and Mac said at the same time.

"Salted fucking fish!"

He quickly opened the next crate and again found the same contents.

"This is so unfair," Jack said from the surface. "What in the fuck is happening down there?"

"We found enough salted fish to feed a third world country for a very long time," Dax said.

"Is that all there is in the hold?" Jack asked.

"It appears to be, at least in this compartment," Dax replied.

He quickly moved his flashlight around the walls of the compartment.

"There are three more hatches, one facing forward, one aft, and one starboard," Dax said.

He knew the starboard door led to the same type of corridor as they had just vacated, and was more than likely flooded from the explosives. He awkwardly maneuvered toward the aft-facing hatch. He stopped in his tracks when he spotted another set of remains, resting in a sitting position on some sort of crate tucked away in the corner. Dax studied the remains, starting at the skull and shoulders. "He must have been some sort of officer," he said. "Look at the gold epaulets resting on his shoulders."

He moved the flashlight further down the skeleton and froze; resting between two ribs was a gold nametag. Dax kneeled down to see if he could get a better look at the name without disturbing the tag. It read, "Boris Smirnov, Ship's Purser."

"Well, I'll be damned," Dax whispered.

"What?" Dona asked.

He didn't answer right away, but moved his light further down. Lo and behold, tightly clutched in the boney hands of the purser, were two shiny gold bars.

"Eureka!" Dax whispered. "Guys," he said as he held the flashlight on the prize. "Do you see what I see?"

"Oh boy, do I see," Dona said. "Mac?"

"Hell yeah, I see," he replied. "I think we may have found what we've been looking for, ladies and gentlemen."

Dax continued moving the light further down and stopped again when he saw, between the skeleton's legs, the dial to a safe. *The purser is sitting on a fucking safe.*

"We're listening, Dax, what did you find?" a familiar voice said from the surface.

"I hear you, Jack. Uh, we found the rest of the *purser's journals,*" he said, being as discreet as possible.

Everyone heard Brad yelling in the background.

"How many?" Jack asked over Brad's voice.

"Just a couple," Dax replied. "But I'm sure the rest are here somewhere."

"How's your air supply?" Jack asked.

"Getting low," Dax said. "We're going to surface, change tanks, get more supplies, and get right back down here."

"We'll be waiting," Jack said. "Be careful."

Dax made a last-minute decision and gently removed the two epaulets and the nametag from the remains of the ship's officer, and tucked them into a pocket on his weight belt. *It's only right that I do whatever I can to get these personal effects into the hands of a family member.* Next, he removed the two gold bars and placed them securely inside his BC and started slowly making his way back to the corridor. Again, Mac and Dona helped him through the small hatch, and he secured it behind him.

"Now this next step could be tricky," Dax said. "When we start to open the next hatch, one of two things could happen. Depending on how the hatch was designed, it will begin to leak water as the airtight seal begins to break, or the pressure will force it open immediately when the lock disengages."

"Either way," Mac said. "I can handle it. You guys brace yourself."

Mac stood as far back from the hatch as he could and still reach the handle before he slowly started to turn the wheel. Enormous pressure from the other side of the hatch made the wheel more difficult to turn, but Mac was able to manage it on his own. As he slowly turned the wheel, water started seeping in around the perimeter of the hatch.

"The best possible scenario," Dax said.

Mac turned the wheel a little more until water started spraying through the entire perimeter of the hatch.

"Okay, stop," Dax shouted. "Let's allow the corridor to fill up, and once the pressure levels out, the hatch should easily open." It took about ten minutes for the small corridor to fill with water, and as expected, Mac was able to easily open the hatch door and they were able to swim out of the corridor and to the surface without any trouble. They broke the surface of the water, and Brad and Jack were standing on the swim platform waiting for them.

Even through the full-face dive mask, Dax couldn't hide his smile. One by one, Brad and Jack got everyone on board and their tanks and BC's off. Dax reached into the pocket on his dive belt and pulled out the epaulets and name tag. "Guys, this hasn't seen the light of day in over one hundred years."

Jack took the items from his hands and studied them closely.

"Neither have these," Dax said, and he pulled two gold bars from inside his BC.

Jack's smile was as broad as Dax's. He leaned in and kissed Dax quickly as he took one of the gold bars and kissed it too.

"What's it like down there?" Brad asked.

"It's like stepping back into another world," Dona said. "It felt so strange to be fully suited but be standing in only knee-deep water. We couldn't have imagined that all this time, the inner compartments weren't flooded."

"What about that salted fish?" Jack asked.

"It's the damnedest thing," Dax said. "There are about five hundred cases of the stuff. Why would a ship of this size be carrying five hundred cases of salted fish?"

"What else did you find down there?" Brad asked.

"Guess what the purser was sitting on?" Dax asked.

"No!" Dona said. "The purser's safe?"

"I don't think it's the purser's safe, but it's a safe just the same."

"Why do you not think it's the purser's safe?" Brad asked.

"For starters, the purser's safe is typically located in the chief purser's office and built into the ship's hull for added security," Dax said. "But... during that time, it wasn't uncommon for a wealthy patron to load his or her own personal safe onto a ship if they were making a one-way trip."

"Makes sense to me," Brad said.

"In addition," Dax continued, "it wasn't uncommon for the chief purser to have a secondary safe to serve as a backup for larger items or additional valuables."

"That would probably explain why the ship's purser was guarding the safe," Dona said.

Dax thought for a second. "I would imagine that when the chief purser realized the ship was in trouble, he sent the ship's purser down to the cargo hold to guard the safe until help came," Dax said. "The poor bastard had no idea that he was being sent to his final resting place."

"He was sitting so calmly at his post," Dona said.

"He probably suffocated little by little when the oxygen ran out," Mac added.

"Okay, guys, enough talk about the dead," Dona said. "We have a hell of a lot work to do before this day is out."

"What's the plan?" Jack asked.

"We need to make a list of what we need to take down with us," Dax said. "For starters, I'd like to wear a regular mask and regulator, which would make it so much easier to maneuver once we're back in the hull."

"I agree," Dona said.

"Wait a minute," Jack interrupted. "What about communication?"

"Jack, we've been inside the hull, and we know it's safe," Dax said. "Relax, we'll be fine."

"What if you *do* get into trouble down there," Jack asked. "What then?"

"I didn't realize you were such a worrywart, Jack," Dax said as he lifted his hands to Jack's face in a comforting gesture.

"I never used to be," Jack replied. "So I guess you have yourself to blame for that."

"Okay, how about this?" Dax asked. "We're each taking two tanks, so if we're not back exactly ninety minutes after our descent, you come and get us."

"The problem is that I don't know how to find you," Jack snapped. "I wasn't down there, remember?"

A thought hit Dax immediately. "Problem solved," he said. "Mac shot the entire thing on video. You and Brad can watch the video while we're below and you'll get to see the entire adventure and know exactly where to find us if something goes wrong."

"I still don't like it," Jack said.

"I know, Jack," Dax said. "But we need flexibility down there, and the smaller masks and regulators will be so much easier to work with."

Dona started gathering tools. Brad changed out the tanks and set up the new BC's and regulators. Mac went in search of a new videotape for the camera to replace the one they'd used when they were under the surface, and Jack stormed off to the bridge. Dax gave Dona a few more things to add to the list, then went in search of Jack. When he reached the bridge, Jack was standing at the helm with the binoculars up to his eyes. *God, he's gorgeous*, Dax thought as he slipped in behind him and slid his arms around Jack's waist.

Jack tensed for a second, then relaxed.

"Any movement over there?" Dax asked.

"None that I can tell," Jack curtly responded. "But the way the wind is blowing, I can't see the stern or the starboard side."

"Don't you think they would have made their move by now if they were monitoring us?" Dax asked.

"I guess so," Jack conceded. "I can't put my finger on it, but something just doesn't feel right about that boat."

"Maybe we're just being paranoid," Dax said as he kissed Jack gently on the neck. "I love you, Jack."

Jack put the binoculars down and turned to face Dax. "I love you too, Dax, that's why I'm so pissed off about not being able to communicate with you. I feel so helpless."

"I know you're pissed, Jack," Dax said. "I can feel it, and I can see it. But if this thing between us is going to work, you're going to have to learn that you can't get your way all the time."

"Is that what you think this is all about?" Jack snapped. "Getting my way?"

"Not really. Well, maybe partly," Dax said shyly. "But listen, Jack, I get it. I know you want to protect me, but I'm not used to being coddled. I've been alone for so long, and that's all I'm used to."

Jack pulled Dax in and held on to him, squeezing him tightly. "Okay, you win," he said.

"It's not about winning or losing," Dax whispered. "But thanks."

Dax heard Dona calling his name over and over. She finally stuck her head on the bridge. "Let's go, Dax!" she yelled.

"I'm on my way, you big dyke," he said. "Stop the damn yelling."

Dona, Dax, and Mac suited up, and Mac made sure they synchronized their watches for exactly ninety minutes below the surface.

"And just so you know," Jack instructed. "If I don't see your smiling faces on the surface in exactly ninety minutes, I'm coming down there to get you. Understood?"

"Yes, sir," they all responded in unison. They put their masks on and started their descent.

"What do you say we go down below and watch that video in case we have to save their sorry asses?" Brad said.

"I think that's a good idea," Jack said. "Is our equipment still ready in case we have to get down there in a hurry?"

"We're good to go," Brad said.

ONCE below the surface, the divers followed their previous route and entered the hull at the same location. This time feeling much lighter and less encumbered, Dax took the lead and was the first to enter the corridor. As they had on the first dive, they were all in the corridor when Mac closed and secured the hatch behind them. Jack again opened the inside hatch, and the water started to slowly recede. When the water was again at their knees, the three of them stepped into the cargo compartment.

Keeping their regulators in their mouths but removing their swim fins for maneuverability, they all made their way to the opposite side of the compartment. Dax approached the forward hatch and tapped his crowbar against it to see if he could pick up a hollow sound, indicating whether the forward compartment was flooded or not. The sound was hollow, and he thought it sounded like an echo, but he wasn't sure.

He looked at Dona and Mac and wished he could ask them their opinion. It was more difficult being down here and not able to communicate with each other as well as with the surface using these normal regulators. He gave Jack the credit he was due and made a mental note to tell him that he was right when they surfaced.

He gave Dona and Mac a questioning look, and they nodded in agreement. He took that as a "go for it." The only good thing was that this hatch opened into the next compartment, so if it was flooded, there was no chance of danger; even if they tried, there would be no opening it against the enormous pressure.

Dax slowly turned the round handle until it stopped.

Here goes nothing! He slowly pushed against the hatch, and much to his surprise, it opened with little resistance. *Dry. Thank you, Lord.*

He stepped into the untouched compartment, shining his flashlight in every direction before cautiously going in any farther. Dona and Mac were right behind him, throwing caution to the wind, but with the three flashlights now illuminating it, the compartment took on an eerie glow.

The first thing Dax spotted was more stacked, wooden crates. *Oh great, more fish.* As with the first set of crates, there was no writing on the outside indicating their contents.

He moved toward the crates and again used his crowbar to break the seal on one of the crates. He pried the lid off and peeked inside. Dona and Mac were looking over his shoulder and they all flashed their light into the crate. The top of the crate was lined with some sort of material, and as he touched it, the material disintegrated under his touch. He brushed the remnants of it aside, and he couldn't believe his eyes.

He let out a yell through his regulator, which probably sounded like a bull in distress, but he didn't care. They all knew what they'd found, and Dona and Mac were jumping up and down with eyes as big as pancakes. At a closer look, the top of each of the shiny gold bars was embedded with a "1lb" stamp. He counted fifty bars in the crate then stepped back to count the total number of crates. *Ten crates in all. That's five hundred pounds of gold.*

He opened a few more of the crates to make sure the contents were the same, and then set out to check out the rest of the compartment. Lying on the floor near the forward hatch was another set of remains. This skeleton appeared to be facedown, but wore the same type of epaulets and nametag as the previous officer. Dax picked up the nametag and read it: "Sergey Popov, Chief Purser."

He showed the name tag to Dona and Mac, and they nodded. He picked up the epaulets and nametag and again placed both in the pocket of his weight belt. Other than the purser's remains and the gold, the compartment was empty. Dax picked up one of the crates and carried it into the other compartment. Dona and Mac followed suit, and within minutes all the crates were in the compartment with them. Dax looked at his watch. A little over an hour had passed, which left them under thirty minutes to complete the operation before Jack and Brad would enter the water and come looking for them.

He signaled for everyone to get back into the corridor, and he closed the hatch behind them. When the hatch was securely closed, Mac again started to slowly open the outside hatch. The cabin once more filled up with water, and when they were totally submerged, he opened the hatch completely. They swam into the next corridor, and one by one approached the blown hole in the ship's hull.

Chapter 13

BRAD and Jack had watched the video of Dax, Dona, and Mac's journey three times, feeling pretty comfortable that they could find them in an emergency. They were just about to turn off the video when Jack moved to the end of the couch and yelled, "Stop the video."

Brad hit the "pause" button on the remote control, and the video stopped.

"Oh my God, Brad," Jack swore. "Do you see what I see?"

As Mac had been filming Dax and Dona leaving the ship, in the background, lurking along the reef line, the camera picked up two divers holding spearguns.

"Holy, Jesus," Brad said as all the blood drained from his face.

"I knew it," Jack said. "They're in danger. I can feel it. We've got to help them."

Jack jumped up from the couch, heading for the companionway door with Brad right behind him, but before they could reach the steps, the door flew open and three armed men entered the salon. "Going somewhere, gentlemen?" the man said in a very strong Russian accent.

Jack's first thought was to get to his gun, but where was it? He quickly looked around the cabin, but remembered that the last time he'd seen it was when he gave it to Brad. The man must have seen Jack weighing his options.

"Is this what you're looking for?" he said as one of his companions held up his forty-five. Jack's heart sank. He gave Brad a "what the fuck?" look, and Brad reached for the waistband of his jeans. Then he remembered. "Fuck fuck fuck," he whispered. He'd put the gun on the table when he was on deck setting up the emergency dive equipment.

Jack's expression changed to one of sympathy, and he quickly turned his attention to the intruder. He appeared to be fairly fit, early seventies maybe, salt and pepper short-cropped hair, with a goatee and glasses. He looked almost refined in an odd sort of way.

"Who are you?" Jack asked.

"My name is Vladimir Kozlov," he said. "I own th—"

Jack stopped him in mid-sentence. "I know what you own."

"You have been doing a little research of your own, I see?" Vladimir said.

"What do you want with us?" Brad asked.

"Captain Cameron, you disappoint me," Vladimir said. "Is this how you treat guests aboard your boat?"

Vladimir turned to Brad and said, "And you must be Dr. Mitchell. Pleased to make your acquaintance."

"Okay," Jack said. "All the niceties are out of the way—what do you want with us?"

"All in good time," Vladimir said. "All in good time. Handcuff them."

Chapter 14

DONA was the first to exit the ship's hull. She put her hands on the hull as she exited to propel herself up and out. Before she could turn around to check on Mac and Dax, her regulator was suddenly ripped out of her mouth, and a hand quickly replaced it. She bit down on the hand as hard as she could, and the intruder released his grip. She felt for her regulator, floating by her side, and stuck it back into her mouth. She felt hands gripping each arm and two spearguns pointing at her side. She turned from left to right, and then she froze as she saw Mac exiting the hull.

Before he was completely out of the hull, someone grabbed his tanks from behind and dragged him up to the top of the wreck. He struggled to turn around and see what was pulling him, but it was useless. When the upward motion stopped, a hand reached around his neck and held a knife to his throat. Much to her surprise, when Dax exited the hull, no one approached him. He swam up, turned, and they both saw the panic in his eyes. The divers motioned for him to surface as they followed closely behind.

When Dax surfaced, two very muscular, armed divers were waiting for him on the swim platform. In one quick motion, they pulled him out of the water by his BC and tanks and stood him on the deck. In a split second, one of his hands was pulled behind his back and a handcuff was slapped around his wrist and attached to the guardrail.

"What the fuck," he said as he spit his regulator out of his mouth and ripped off his mask with the other hand. "Where are Dona and Mac? Where are Jack and Brad?"

"We ask the questions here, *strannyi*," one of the divers said with a heavy Russian accent, and they both laughed. The way they were laughing, Dax thought it must have been Russian for *queer* or *faggot.*

Dona and Mac surfaced with their captors, and Dona pushed toward the back of the boat. In the same quick motion, she was lifted out of the water, placed on the platform, and handcuffed just as Dax had been, and Mac followed suit. Now the three of them were standing on the deck of the boat, handcuffed to the guardrail, not knowing what had hit them. Jack and Brad appeared on deck, handcuffed and with duct tape across their mouths, with Vladimir and his two thugs.

"Oh my God! Jack…. Brad, are you okay?" Dax asked.

Jack and Brad nodded to Dax.

"Nicely done," Vladimir said to one of the divers when he saw Dax, Dona, and Mac handcuffed to the guardrail.

Dax looked at Vladimir. "Who the fuck are you?" he demanded.

"Such language, Mr. Powers," Vladimir said. "Where are your manners?"

"Fuck my manners," Dax said. "Why in the hell are you holding us against our will?"

"You have something that belongs to me, Mr. Powers, and I expect you to give it to me," Vladimir said.

Playing dumb, and doing everything to not let on that they had the gold, Dax said, "What in the fuck are you talking about?"

Vladimir laughed. "Don't play dumb with me, Mr. Powers. I've been monitoring your radio contact for quite some time now," he said. "If you insist on continuing this little charade, I'll have to take it out on your little sister."

Jack looked at Dona. "Okay! Okay," he said. "Just don't hurt her."

"Dax, don't," Dona said.

"All we found were some cans of salted fish and some ship's journals," Dax said in one last attempt to hold onto the gold.

"And no gold," Vladimir said. "I think not."

Vladimir nodded to one of his divers, and the diver unlocked Dona's handcuffs and walked her over to the edge of the deck, then put his knife at her throat.

"No!" Dax shouted. His poker face was now gone. Any hopes he'd had of bluffing his way out of this were now long gone. "I'll tell you anything you want to know."

"How many cans of salted fish are down there?" Vladimir asked.

"My best guess is about five hundred cases," Dax replied.

"How many cans are packed to a case?" Vladimir asked.

"Six, I think," Dax said.

Vladimir did the math. *That's three thousand pounds.* A broad smile consumed his face.

"I'm sure you are wondering why an old man like me would get so excited about so many cans of fish," Vladimir said. "But let us get them on board and I'll tell you all about it."

Vladimir looked out onto the canal and saw his boat heading toward them.

"I hope you don't mind, Captain Cameron, but I have instructed my crew to dock my boat along your port side while Mr. Powers takes my divers down and shows them where they can find my fish—oh, and my gold," he laughed. "And one more thing. Do not get any ideas about doing anything crazy. If you do, I will personally kill your companions, starting with your sister, and then your boyfriend. Do I make that perfectly clear, Mr. Powers?"

Dax nodded in agreement.

"Now get your tanks and full face mask back on," Vladimir ordered as he headed to the bridge to radio his boat. "If you force me to kill your companions, I want you to hear them suffer one by one." Vladimir stopped. "And get the others' mouths taped shut. I don't want them talking to one another."

"Wait!" Dax shouted. Vladimir stopped again and turned to Dax. "Make it quick," he said.

"Before we go back down, I need to blow the hull in order to flood the compartment where the crates of gold and salted fish are being stored. If we don't blow the hull, it will take days to get the crates out using the current method of entering and exiting the hull."

Vladimir considered his statement with some apprehension. "Take my divers down, and show them what you want to do. If they agree with your assessment, I will do as you say."

Finally! Dax thought. *A break—this may be the only chance I have to save us.*

DAX took his good old time suiting up. He was purposely stalling, trying to buy a little time to come up with a plan. He took a quick inventory of Vladimir's men. There were three divers and two guards, plus Vladimir. Dax assumed that the three divers would accompany him under the surface and the guards would remain topside to watch over the others. He and Jack locked eyes, and the overwhelming helplessness Jack was feeling was evident in his stare. Dax tried to show him that there was still hope, but he didn't have much hope himself. *Think, Dax, think! Okay, if I could somehow get the divers into the interior compartment and seal them in, their tanks would eventually run out of air and they would suffocate. That would leave the two guards and Vladimir. But what about Vladimir's boat? He could have another twenty crew members on board.*

Dax's mind continued from one scenario to the next. Every scenario presented another question. Every possible solution presented another problem. By the time Dax finished suiting up, he felt thoroughly defeated. *I won't give up. I just can't.*

Not sure of what he was going to do next, Dax smiled at the others and mouthed, "I'm sorry! I love you." Their eyes told him everything he needed to know. He turned and walked down the stairs to the swim platform where his escorts were waiting for him. Dax stepped off the swim platform and began his descent, surrounded by the three divers.

JACK'S mind was racing. *This is not his fault. Why is he apologizing? I've got to do something. If I could just get to the dinghy, but what then?* He looked over at the others, and he could tell they were all thinking the same thing.

Minutes later, Vladimir's boat pulled alongside the *Lindsey C.* Four crewmembers secured the two boats together, and Vladimir boarded his boat. He calmly sat on deck and smoked a Cuban cigar and drank Russian vodka while he waited for his divers to return with a sample of his gold and salted fish.

Jack was still trying to make sense out of all of this. Vladimir was more interested in the salted fish than the gold, but why? *What can he want with three thousand pounds of salted fish? What's so damn great about… unless it's not salted fish at all?*

DONA'S mind was doing backflips. She wished like hell she could talk to the guys to see if they had any ideas, but it was totally impossible to communicate with their hands securely cuffed to the guardrail behind them and duct tape across their mouths. They were cuffed so closely to one another that they were touching, but if they weren't able to communicate, they might as well have been a million miles away. So for all intents and purposes, they were on their own to try and make heads or tails out of their situation. Dona thought about her brother. At this point everything depended on him, and she ached for him. *Why should he be the one to carry the burden of all of this? We're all in this together. It's not his fault.*

Chapter 15

DAX led the dive team to the blown entrance of the wreck, although he didn't know why he bothered. After all, they had apprehended him, Mac, and Dona at that same spot when they were coming out of the wreck, and he was sure they could have found it on their own. He showed them the open corridor hatch and said, "In there."

The first diver cleared the hatch, and then the second. "Now you," the third diver said with a heavy Russian accent.

It's now or never. His only plan was to force the third diver into the hatch and close it behind them. He would slip his crowbar into the wheel handle and jam it up against the interior wall of the ship. That would lock the wheel in place and keep them inside the corridor. He knew that they could exit through the hatch facing forward, which opened into the next corridor, and they could escape through one of the blown hulls. But he didn't know if they knew that, and this plan, at the very least, would buy him some time.

Dax made his move. He knew it would take the other two divers a reasonable amount of time to make their way back out of the corridor if they saw the struggle, so he felt better knowing the odds were now even—it was one against one. The diver was behind him, urging him forward through the hatch. He spread his legs as wide as he could to stop himself from going through the hatch, ripped the crowbar from his dive belt, and rammed it behind him into the stomach of the Russian diver. He heard the thump as well as the diver's gasp in response to the blow. Unfortunately, so did the other divers, who then started scrambling for their spearguns. As Dax struggled with his opponent, he fought to keep an eye on the other two through the array of air bubbles escaping everyone's dive apparatus. One of the divers made his way to the entrance of the hatch with his speargun cocked and ready. He aimed it at Dax, and Dax did the only thing he could think to do—use his opponent as a shield.

The Russian diver pulled the trigger, and the spear released just as Dax spun his opponent around. Dax was looking directly into the eyes of the Russian, who seemed to know exactly what was happening. Dax knew the second the Russian realized that he'd been shot. He saw the disbelief, fear, and pain register when the spear entered his back and came out of his chest. Dax felt a warm sensation and then a burst of pain. He looked down and saw that the spear had gone through the Russian and lodged into his right shoulder. In a panic, he forced the Russian diver away from him, which in turn, pulled the spear out of his shoulder. He bellowed in pain as the diver floated away from him with no signs of life.

By now, the other two divers were out of the corridor and had each of his arms secured. Dax was resigned to the fact that he'd lost. He'd tried, but he'd lost. The pain was overwhelming and he was beginning to feel lightheaded. His last thoughts before he lost consciousness were of Jack, Dona, Mac, and Brad. *I'm sorry I couldn't save you!*

JACK watched Vladimir move to the stern of his boat. He looked in their direction and said, "It appears that your boyfriend is not as smart as I thought he was."

The divers broke the surface of the water, carrying Dax. Blood was pouring out of the gaping hole in his right shoulder. Jack was the first to see his lover lifelessly floating on the surface. No duct tape could silence the gut-wrenching wail of pain that escaped Jack's mouth. Dona turned white and fell to her knees as she fainted. Mac and Brad dropped next to her, but in their situation, there was nothing that could be done. Jack started ripping and pulling at the guardrail in an attempt to break free and get to Dax, but it was no use. The force of his efforts tore the skin on his wrists and they began to bleed heavily. Realizing he'd failed, he, too, sunk to his knees.

"Get him on board," Vladimir shouted to his divers. "I want him alive and conscious to witness the death of his lover, his sister, and his friends."

The divers dragged Dax on board the *Lindsey C* and dropped him next to Jack. Jack looked at Brad, his mind pleading with him to help, but he knew Brad could do no more than he could. In Jack's mind, he started begging Vladimir to allow Brad to help Dax. He'd never begged anyone for anything in his entire life, but he would gladly do it now if it could save Dax. He got as close as he could to the still-motionless Dax. His legs were all that could reach him, but he needed to touch him, to feel him. In his mind, he ordered Dax to hold on, *please just hold on.* But hold on for what, Jack didn't know.

"Well, Mr. Cleary, since Ms. Powers appears to be out of commission, you're next on the food chain," Vladimir said. "No funny business this time or they all die, execution-style."

Mac started mumbling through his taped mouth.

"Remove the tape," Vladimir ordered.

The guard reached over and ripped the tape from Mac's mouth.

"Fuck!" Mac shouted from the pain. "Brad's a doctor, please let him help Dax," he pleaded.

"And prolong the inevitable?" Vladimir said. "Why?"

Resigned to the fact that they probably were not going to get out of this situation alive, Mac took a deep breath and looked at Brad. "I love you, Brad. No one can take that away from us."

Brad nodded as tears began to run down his cheeks.

Mac turned to Vladimir. "Let them go, and I will do whatever you want. I will salvage the entire wreck myself and you can leave me down there to die. I don't really care what you do to me, but please, just let them go."

"How brave of you, Mr. Cleary," Vladimir said. "Your mother must be so proud. But I do not deal unless I absolutely have to, and the way I see it, I have the complete upper hand here."

Mac opened his mouth to speak, but Vladimir put his hand up to stop him.

"Yes, I know… I'm down one diver, but look." He pointed at three men on the back of his boat. "I have three more on standby, awaiting my command. So with all due respect, no, I will not let them go."

"If you're going to kill us anyway," Mac protested, "why should I bother taking your divers into the wreck?"

"There are many ways to die, Mr. Cleary," Vladimir explained. "One way would be quick and painless. But another way could be long and very, very painful. Which would you prefer?"

"You win," Mac said.

"I always win," Vladimir said. "Now get him suited up."

The guard unlocked Mac's handcuffs and escorted him to the other side of the deck, where he held him at gunpoint while he suited up. When Mac was suited, he again looked over at Brad. There really wasn't anything left to say. He walked down the steps of the swim platform to reach the original two divers, who were joined now by a third and awaiting his arrival. He looked back and saw Dona and Dax, still unconscious, lying next to Jack and Brad, handcuffed to the guardrail. *I can't believe it's going to end like this.* He turned and jumped into the water.

Chapter *16*

THIS time there was no plan. Mac was out of options, and he didn't want anyone to suffer a long, painful death, so he did as he was told. They entered the corridor, and Mac followed the same procedure they'd followed previously. While one diver guarded him, the other two divers carried a crate of gold and a crate labeled "Salted Fish" into the corridor. Mac explained that the explosives were already set up on the opposite wall of the compartment, and they would need to detonate the explosives to flood the cabin in order to get the crates out more easily.

They returned to the corridor and exited the wreck the way they entered it. Again, one diver guarded Mac while the other two each carried a small crate. The divers inflated their BC's when they exited the wreck to help them surface with the added weight, and they effortlessly floated to the surface. Vladimir had been monitoring their conversations, and when Mac surfaced, he was awaiting their arrival with the smile of a child on Christmas morning. Two of the guards lifted the crates up to the swim platform and then carried them to the deck and placed them at Vladimir's feet.

Mac, held at gunpoint, watched as Vladimir instinctively lifted the lid off the unmarked crate containing the six cans of salted fish. He took a knife from one of the divers and stabbed the top of the can, making a hole big enough to get his finger in. He stuck his finger in his mouth to wet it and then slid it inside the can. He removed his finger and held it against his tongue and sampled the contents. Vladimir smiled, set the can down on the table, and opened the second crate. During the ascent, the water had swept away any signs of protective material, so all he saw when he lifted the lid were bars of shiny gold.

Mac looked over at Jack, Dona—who was now conscious—and Brad, watching the events unfold. They all had confused looks on their faces, but of course none of them could speak.

"If we're all going to die," Mac said. "Can you at least tell us what we are dying for?"

Vladimir, now in a very good mood, took a deep breath.

"The *Anna Wyoming* was owned and operated by one of Russia's strongest and most notorious drug cartels. The ship's captain, Viktor Kozlov, was my grandfather and also a drug lord for the cartel. His responsibility, along with the chief purser and ship's purser—also in the cartel—was to make the Lynn Canal run to Skagway once a month, smuggling Chinese opium into the United States through Russia."

"So that's three thousand pounds of opium down there," Mac said. "How much is that worth?"

"About forty million dollars in today's market," Vladimir responded.

Dax started to moan and opened his eyes. Jack could see the pain in Dax's face, but much to his surprise, Dax inched himself in Jack's direction and propped himself up on his chest.

"Do you want the story or not?" Vladimir asked.

Mac looked at the guys. Anything to stall. "Yes, sorry!"

"Where was I?" Vladimir said to himself. "Oh, yes. This was the biggest run the cartel had ever attempted," he explained. "As a matter of fact, it was so big, and the cartel was so worried about its cargo, that the ship's purser and the chief purser were ordered to remain in the cargo hold to guard the opium and were not allowed to leave their post for the entire journey."

"That explains the remains we found," Mac said.

"Remains?" Vladimir asked.

Mac attempted to walk over to Dax, but the guard stopped him. Mac looked at Vladimir and asked, "Can I show you something?"

"Don't try anything foolish," he replied.

Mac reached down into Dax's dive belt and removed the nametags and the epaulets he'd brought to the surface. He stood and brought them to Vladimir.

Vladimir looked at the gold items closely and held them tightly in his hands against his chest. "They were my great uncle's," he said. He bowed his head and made the sign of the cross. He laid the items on the table next to the opium and continued his story.

"Because of the Klondike Gold Rush," Vladimir said, "the cartel also started smuggling gold out of the country, for wealthy drug customers who wanted to avoid the high export taxes affiliated with shipping the gold out through normal channels. The fact that there was so much gold on board this ship was just an added bonus," he explained. "There were rumors, of course, that the ship was carrying gold, but the cartel had no documented record of such cargo on board, so we did not believe that the rumors held any merit.

"My grandfather had dedicated his entire life to the success of the cartel, and when his own ship went down with so much opium on board, he feared that the cartel, as well as his reputation and his family name, would be ruined. The night of the tragedy, the cartel ordered that he leave the ship immediately and take with him exact coordinates and the purser's journal and lay low until the wreck was a distant memory. Someday they would find the wreck and retrieve our bounty. But before my grandfather could deliver the journal and coordinates to the cartel, he was killed. Some say it was an internal job for threatening the existence of the cartel, but I do not believe that theory. The cartel wanted the information he had—why would they kill him? Either way, the journal or coordinates were never found until you stumbled upon them."

So someone did *survive, and that's how we got the information,* Dona thought, wishing she could speak.

"Eventually, my father, Aleksandr Kozlov, was appointed to head the cartel, and he dedicated his entire life to finding those documents in an attempt to recover the opium, and in the process, restore his father's good name. But, unfortunately, he never succeeded. When my father's health started to deteriorate, I became head of the cartel, which is alive and well and now controlling most of the world's international drug trade. But on his deathbed, I promised to continue his efforts, and I, too, have dedicated my life to doing just that."

Silence overtook the deck of the boat, and then Vladimir clapped his hands and stood.

"Up until now, I had pretty much resigned myself to the fact that I would never find the documents or the wreck in my lifetime. That is, until I received a call from a cartel insider at the State Office, who told me you had turned up with coordinates and pretty good proof that you had found the wreck. We have been closely monitoring your comings and goings and your progress almost the entire expedition."

"So you broke into our boat to look for the documents while we were away?" Mac asked.

"Now why would we do that, when all we had to do was sit back and let you do the work and we then could reap the rewards?" Vladimir responded. "We stayed as far away from you as we could, to not alert you to the fact that we were onto you."

Mac looked at Jack. "Then who broke into our boat?" Mac asked.

"Who cares?" Vladimir said. "Enough of this small talk. Take them down below, and kill them."

"Wait!" Mac said. "Do you think they won't find us murdered in our boat? The State Office knows we're here," he continued.

"By the time they find your bodies," Vladimir said. "We will be safely out of the country and nearing our homeland. Now kill them, and get back up here and start salvaging my opium and gold."

The guards unlocked the handcuffs and brought Dona and Brad down first. Dax couldn't walk, but they allowed Jack and Mac to carry him, with Vladimir on his heels.

"Can we at least say our good-byes?" Mac asked Vladimir.

Vladimir nodded, and the guards removed the tape from their mouths. They all hung on to one another and huddled around Dax lying on the floor, his shoulder still bleeding pretty badly. Jack kissed Dax on the lips and whispered, "I love you."

"I love you too, Captain," Dax said, his voice very weak. "More than you will ever know."

Dax smiled up at Dona. "It's been a good run, baby sis," he said. "I wouldn't have wanted to do it with anyone but you. I love you." She only nodded as tears streamed down her face. Mac and Brad didn't say anything. They simply stared into each other's eyes, their looks saying everything they couldn't bring their lips to say.

Dax held up his good arm and smiled. He slipped his hand into Jack's and held on tight. In reaction, Dona took Jack's, Mac hers, and Brad his. In one deliberate last show of unity, Brad reached down to Dax's right arm, lying still at his side, and joined their hands. They all kneeled directly behind Dax and faced their executioner.

The act didn't go unnoticed, and Vladimir yelled, "Enough! Kill them."

The two guards raised their arms and aimed at Jack and Dona first. But before they could pull the trigger, the companionway door flew open, and they all heard, "DEA, drop your weapons and put your hands where we can see them!"

They all watched as six heavily armed agents of the United States Drug Enforcement Agency rushed into the salon and overpowered their captors.

"We need medical assistance right away!" Jack yelled. "Dax, just hold on, baby. We're gonna make it."

Chapter 17

As Jack cradled Dax's head in his arms, he vaguely heard one of the agents radio for medical backup. Within minutes, two Coast Guard paramedics were examining Dax, while two others were sliding a backboard underneath him.

"Where are you taking him?" Dona asked.

"We're transporting him to the *Jolly Roger*, idling just off of your stern," the paramedic responded. "A Coast Guard cutter will be here in less than ten minutes."

"I'm going with him," Jack demanded.

"Me too," Dona said.

"We're all going," Mac said, still holding Brad's hand.

Another agent stepped into the salon and said, "I'm Agent Brett Wilder. Please give them a few minutes to stabilize him, and then I'll personally take you to be with him."

"You're the guy from the State Office," Dona said.

"State Office, thank God," Vladimir said. "I am a Russian citizen being held against my will, and I demand to be returned to my country."

"I'm sorry, sir, but I'm afraid it will be a long time before you see Russia," Agent Wilder said.

"You can't hold me against my will," Vladimir protested.

"We can, sir, and we will," Agent Wilder said. "For starters, you are being arrested for drug trafficking, drug possession, kidnapping, and attempted murder." He instructed another agent, "Read him his rights."

The agent started reading Vladimir his rights.

"I need air," Jack said as he climbed the stairs to the deck. Dona, Mac, and Brad followed, and when they reached the deck, they were greeted by the sight of Vladimir's guards, the captain and crew of his boat, and all the divers handcuffed to the same guardrail that had held them a little over an hour ago.

When the agent was finished reading him his rights, Vladimir was also escorted topside and was greeted by the same sight. Dona walked up to Vladimir and kicked him in the balls as hard as she could. "That's for my brother," she said as she turned and walked back to join her friends.

They all watched the blood drain from his face as he bent over and fell to his knees. Agent Wilder flinched and said, "You shouldn't have done that, ma'am."

"I'm sorry, Agent Wilder," she responded.

"Okay, just don't let it happen again," he said with a chuckle.

Chapter *18*

SO MUCH had happened in a very short time that everyone's head was spinning.

"How did you find us?" Jack asked.

"We've been involved from the beginning, although quite by accident," Agent Wilder explained. "We've been secretly monitoring the comings and goings of Mr. Kozlov for over two years, and working to gather enough information to make our move."

They listened intently as Wilder continued to explain.

"I know that you're aware that our Mr. Kozlov is the head of one of Russia's largest and most powerful drug cartels."

Jack nodded but asked, "How did you know that *we* knew that?"

"Every cabin of your vessel has been bugged since you left the State Office," Wilder explained. "We had to know what your plans were so we could protect you, but we knew that Kozlov wouldn't go anywhere near you if he got wind of our involvement, so we stayed out of sight."

"So you're the ones who broke into the boat while we were away," Brad said.

"Yes, sir," Wilder confessed. "Sorry for the mess, but we tried to figure out a way to alert you to the fact that you were being monitored without compromising our mission."

"Well, it worked," Mac and Jack said simultaneously.

"And you owe us for new underwear," Brad said as he looked at Dona. "But we'll talk about that later, go on."

"I'm not really sure where to start, so I guess I'll start at the beginning," Wilder said. "The wreck of the *Anna Wyoming* is very well known around these parts, and the rumors have run rampant for over one hundred years about what she was carrying, but no one could prove anything until recently. We've had an agent that poses as a clerk at the State Office and has been working for the last ten years to infiltrate the cartel and act as our informant, and just recently he verified that the ship was carrying at least three thousand pounds of opium. Anyway, it was pure coincidence that I happened to be in the State Office the day you came to apply for your Rights of Salvage. When the desk clerk heard which wreck you were after, she immediately brought it to my attention, and we thought we had finally gotten the break we needed. So we fast-tracked your certificate and bugged your boat before you could get back to it."

"So you heard everything that Vladimir said about his father, the cartel, and the night of the wreck?" Jack asked.

"Thanks to Mr. Cleary, we have enough on tape to put Mr. Kozlov away for a very long time," Wilder explained. "And once he sees what he's facing, I'm sure he'll start singing like a bird."

"I hope that bastard rots in prison for his part in what happened to Dax," Dona said.

"I promise you that we will do our very best to make sure that happens," Wilder said. "I know you don't believe me, but there was very little danger of any of you getting hurt. We were on the *Jolly Roger* and very close to you the entire time, but knew that if we brought in a cutter, Mr. Kozlov would have run, and we would have lost him."

"Tell that to Dax," Dona said.

"I know, ma'am, and I'm sorry about that. We were aware of what had happened to Dax as soon as it happened, and had doctors evaluating the situation from the moment the shot was fired."

"Yeah, knowing that now is great," Mac said. "But it sure would have helped to know that when all this was going down."

"I'm sorry about that, but it couldn't be helped," Agent Wilder confessed.

"What about the gold?" Dona asked.

"It's yours," Wilder said. "It's the least we can do."

Everyone smiled, and Jack said, "Please take us to Dax."

"Right away, sir!" Wilder said.

ONCE they were all on board the Coast Guard cutter, Brad went to talk to the doctors about Dax's prognosis. Jack stood on one side of Dax's bed, tightly holding his hand, with Dona on the other side and Mac at his feet. They took their time explaining to Dax about the DEA's involvement in their expedition and how it had all come to be. They had just finished the story when Brad pulled back the curtain and appeared at the foot of the bed.

"Looks like you're going to make a full recovery," Brad said. "Although you lost a considerable amount of blood, the spear didn't do any major damage. After you heal, you'll have to endure some physical therapy to get your range of motion back, but you'll be good as new."

Jack leaned down to kiss Dax on the lips, but Dax stopped him in midair.

"What about the gold?" he asked.

"It's yours," Jack said.

Dax corrected him. "You mean ours." He looked around and smiled at his friends—no, not his friends. His family!

Chapter *19*

IT TOOK the government about a week to complete the salvage of the gold and opium and another week for the DEA to wrap up all the loose ends surrounding the expedition. When everything was signed, sealed, and delivered, the government wired a little over ten million dollars into Dax's bank account, and the ordeal was just about behind them. The DEA salvaged the chief purser's safe and the additional safe and promised to turn over the contents once they sorted through the red tape.

The *Lindsey C* was again docked in her slip in the Skagway harbor, and everyone was sitting comfortably in the salon, enjoying their last meal together before departing for home. The wine was flowing, and everyone was reflecting on their adventure.

Dax stood and tapped a butter knife against his wine glass. "Can I have your attention?" he said. "Dona and I discussed this earlier today, and we want you to have these." He handed Jack, Mac, and Brad each an envelope. Jack's envelope contained a check for two million dollars, and Mac's and Brad's each contained a check for one million.

"I know this isn't what everyone agreed on," Dax said. "But we wanted you each to have a little extra from us. We would have split the gold five ways, but we still have a new boat to pay for, and because of this money, we won't have to rely on investors to fund our expeditions for the foreseeable future."

Jack, Mac, and Brad were dead silent as they stared at their checks.

"Somebody please say something," Dax said.

"I can't accept this," Jack said.

"Why not?" Dona and Dax asked in unison.

"Because I got way more than I needed when I got Dax, and I'm very happy with that."

Everyone smiled and said "Ahhh." Dax leaned down and kissed Jack. "But a deal's a deal," he said. "Besides, if our next few expeditions don't produce any revenue, we may need it."

Mac said, "We don't know what to say."

"Don't say anything," Dona said. "You earned it."

"Thank you," they both said.

"No, thank *you*!" Dax said.

The team knew they would see each other again in the future, because they'd all agreed to testify against Vladimir Kozlov when the case came to trial, and they were all eager to do that.

"What are your plans, Jack?" Mac asked.

"We'll be here a few more days," Jack said, "getting the *Lindsey C* ready to sell. Then we head down to Key West to supervise the construction of the new boat."

"Wow," Brad said. "Uncle Jack's all grown up."

"Very funny, asshole," Jack replied.

"How about you guys?" Dax asked.

"We're flying back up to the lake to spend a few weeks recharging our batteries until we decide on our next adventure," Brad said.

"Would you guys consider making your next adventure a trip to Cape Horn?" Dax asked.

Everyone looked at Dax and Dona in surprise. "The *Sarah Maria*?" they all squealed.

Dax and Dona nodded.

Brad and Mac looked at each other and smiled. "Hell yeah, we're in," they said.

"You know I'm in," Jack said. "When do we leave?"

"Slow down, Captain," Dax said. "We've got to get the boat built before we can do anything, but in the meantime, we have a shitload of research to do."

There were hugs all around as they toasted to their new adventure and turned in for the evening.

Jack opened the cabin door for Dax, and they both stepped inside. When Jack closed the door behind him and turned, Dax was already starting the bodily assault.

"Whoa, whoa," Jack said. "Are you well enough for this?"

He took Jack's cheeks in his hands and brought their lips together as the gentle waves lapped against the hull in an accompaniment to their kiss. Jack felt everything slip away—the expedition, almost losing Dax, almost being killed. It was all replaced by Dax's beautiful hazel eyes, the taste of his lips, and his manly scent.

Jack whimpered softly as the kiss intensified. He felt Dax moving closer and a hand gently stroking his back. Slowly Dax pulled away, studying Jack's face, fingers caressing his cheek, and Jack shivered at the soft touch, leaning closer and wanting more. Jack took Dax's hand and walked him to the bed. Jack kissed him again and said, "I want *you* inside *me* tonight." Dax nodded slowly against his lips. Jack felt rather than saw Dax's smile just before Dax pushed him onto the bed.

Jack held on as they continued kissing, his strong back pressing into the mattress, Dax's weight surrounding him. Jack wrapped his arms around Dax's neck and buried his face in the warm softness of Dax's skin.

"We don't have to do this if you're not ready," Dax whispered. "The last thing I would ever do is pressure you."

"I almost lost you before we had a chance to share this experience," Jack confessed. "I want you, Dax, and I want you tonight." He looked up at Dax and gazed into his eyes. "I trust you, and I know you wouldn't do anything to hurt me."

Jack's eyes were filled with love and trust, and suddenly Dax was overtaken with emotion. He was the first man Jack had ever had sex with, and now Jack was going to allow him to be his first again. A single tear slid down his cheek, and Jack wiped it away with his thumb.

"You okay, baby?" Jack asked.

"I'm better than okay," he whispered. "I never knew I could love someone as much as I love you." Jack shook with excitement as Dax gently placed his lips against Jack's and held them there. It felt like the most sensual, the most real kiss he'd ever shared with anyone, and he was so glad it was Dax.

"Sit up, and let me undress you." Jack did what he was told, and Dax pulled the T-shirt over his head. He gently nudged him back down and slid to the end of the bed. He removed Jack's sneakers and socks. He used his thumbs to sensually rub the balls of Jack's feet, one at a time. He lovingly nibbled on his toes and ran his tongue up and down the soles of Jack's feet until he felt Jack shiver from what he hoped was anticipation. He straddled Jack's thighs and slowly unbuttoned the fly of his "Lucky" brand jeans. *These really are lucky jeans—lucky for me, that is*, he thought as he slid them off and tossed them to the floor. He slipped his fingers inside the waistband of Jack's boxers and slid them down and off as well.

"Roll onto your stomach and just relax." Dax felt Jack shake again as he rolled over and rested his head on his hands. Dax straddled his legs and ran his hands up to the wide planes of Jack's broad shoulders. He dropped his head and whispered, "Don't worry, Captain, just relax and let me take care of you. If I hurt you in any way, just let me know, and I will stop, okay?"

Nervously, Jack nodded. Dax slid his hands back down Jack's back, stopping and kneading the globes of his firm butt. When he dropped his head, Dax saw his own erect dick, wet with the sticky precursor of his anticipated climax as it rested in the crack of Jack's ass. He was so excited that he thought he might lose it right then and there, but he forced himself to calm down, remembering that he wanted to make this special for his captain.

Dax leaned forward and began kissing Jack's back and neck. He teasingly kissed all the way down his back and nibbled on his butt. He felt Jack shiver and tense just for a second, when he parted his ass cheeks and slid his tongue into the warm, welcoming crack. Dax slid his tongue down the cleft and over the opening, and Jack, unfamiliar with the sensation, arched his back. Dax moved his tongue a little, and Jack's head lolled back as he allowed himself to moan softly. Dax repeated the onslaught, this time zeroing in on the small, puckered opening, savoring it with his tongue, Jack's unique scent filling his nose and mouth.

"Dax, oh mannn!" Dax saw this affirmation as an invitation to continue. He probed more deeply, attempting to relax Jack's muscle, parting his cheeks even further as he dove heart-first into the man he'd fallen so in love with. Dax suddenly felt a sense of urgency sweep over him. *Hurry or you're going to wake up and this will all be over.*

He quickly took hold of his senses and realized that Jack wasn't going anywhere. He had his entire life to get this right, and above all, he wanted Jack to enjoy this exploration into his new world. Jack started moving his hips, rubbing his dick against the linens. Dax reached under Jack's torso and grabbed his dick and lightly stroked it. Jack lifted his hips up further to allow Dax ample space to move.

"Are you okay?" Dax asked.

"Oh yeah, but if you don't stop rubbing my dick, I'm going to blow," Jack whispered.

"Not yet, Captain. Your journey has just begun."

Dax released Jack's throbbing dick and slowly slipped his hand out as he reached for the lube on the bedside table. He squeezed a liberal amount onto his finger and spread it around Jack's hole. Dax felt Jack tense up again and shiver a little.

"You okay, Captain?"

"Yeah," Jack responded.

Dax moved his index finger around Jack's opening a few times then slowly slid it inside, up to the first knuckle. He felt Jack's entire body tense with anticipation.

"Hurt?" Dax asked.

"Not really, just feels very strange," Jack replied.

Dax slowly began to move his finger in and out, massaging Jack's insides. Jack seemed to relax, and the tension around Dax's finger relaxed as well. He cautiously added his middle finger and allowed Jack to accept it, too, before he started moving again. This time Jack didn't tense up, and seemed to welcome the invasion. Jack was so tight, and Dax almost shot his load for the second time, imagining how the warmth of Jack's hole would feel surrounding his dick.

Dax slowly started to move in and out, twisting his fingers, searching for the one spot that he knew would make Jack see stars and make this all worth it. Jack started to relax into the pleasurable assault until Dax found what he was searching for. Suddenly Jack lifted completely off of the bed and pushed up onto his knees as he cried out, "Oh my God, I don't know what you just did, but please do it again."

Dax smiled and began to massage Jack's prostate over and over, being rewarded with moans of ecstasy each time he applied any pressure.

Jack looked at Dax over his left shoulder. "If this is what it feels like to… well, you know." He was too embarrassed say the words "get fucked." "I want you now."

Dax smiled at Jack's shyness. "Roll over," he whispered.

Jack did as he was told, and Dax lifted Jack's legs over his shoulders, careful not to aggravate his wound. Opening the small foil package he'd retrieved from the bedside table, Dax slid the condom on, applied a little more lubricant to the condom, and aligned with Jack's entrance.

Knowing how difficult it was for Jack to give up all control, Dax instructed him to place his hands on Dax's thighs and use them to help guide him until he felt comfortable enough to relax. "That way I can feel if you want more or I should slow down," Dax instructed.

Jack nodded, then inhaled and gasped as Dax slid the head of his erect dick slowly inside of his body. Jack felt the stretch and burn consume his body immediately, and stopped Dax from entering any further until he could adjust to the intrusion.

"Jesus, that hurts," Jack admitted, breathing heavily.

"Only for a second, baby, I promise," Dax said. "Just breathe. It'll all be worth it."

When Jack's muscles began to relax around Dax, he took a deep breath, and Dax felt his hands urge him to enter a little further.

Dax did as directed and pushed until he felt Jack stop him again, allowing himself more time to adjust. However, with each push, Dax could feel Jack loosen up and start to accept him. The next time Jack nudged him forward, Dax sank into Jack's body until he couldn't go any further, and leaned in and passionately kissed his lover.

"Just be still for a moment," Jack whispered.

Dax froze and kissed Jack again, exploring the inside of his mouth while his dick was lodged tightly into Jack's ass.

Dax broke the kiss and stared deeply into Jack's eyes. A single tear slipped down his cheek as he whispered "God, you're beautiful. I love you, Jack."

"I love you too, Dax. Now move."

Without breaking eye contact with his lover, Dax watched Jack's sweat-covered expression go from apprehension to amazement.

"Jesus, Dax, this feels so good."

"I know, isn't it incredible? And it only gets better with practice," Dax chuckled.

Still staring into each other's eyes, their bodies moved in a spectacular rhythm as Dax thrust in and out of his lover. He loved the way Jack's muscles felt underneath him as they moved in unison. He explored every inch of Jack that he could reach until his hand landed on Jack's rock-hard dick. He gently stroked in time with his thrusts.

"Oh my God, Dax, every nerve ending is on fire. So many sensations, I can't hold back any longer."

Dax saw Jack's eyes close and felt his muscles tighten around him. His back arched, his head rolled, and he felt Jack's entire body tense. With only a soft whimper, he came in Dax's hand. The sight of Jack, so vulnerable, so trusting, pulled his own climax from deep within Dax's soul, and he instantly filled the condom deep inside Jack's body.

Jack opened his eyes and saw Dax staring down at him, sated and smiling. He reached up and threw his arms around Dax's neck and pulled Dax on top of him. He felt Dax slip out of him, and he felt suddenly empty.

Dax fell alongside Jack and tried to catch his breath. When he was finally able to speak, he said, "When we're out of here, I'm gonna miss this boat, and especially this cabin. This is where it all started," he continued.

"I know how you feel," Jack confessed, knowing that he would give up the *Lindsey C* a hundred times if it meant he got to be with Dax.

They fell asleep in that position, both men content and so in love.

Chapter 20

EARLY the next morning, Dona took a cab into town to rent a truck to get all the equipment back to Portland, while the guys stayed behind to pack everything up. When Dona retuned, they loaded the containers onto the truck, and when everything was packed up tight for the journey, Dona started saying her good-byes. "I'll see you guys as soon as the new boat's ready, if not before," she said to Mac and Brad.

"I'll see you guys in Key West in about two weeks," she said as she hugged Dax and Jack good-bye. "Take care of my brother, Jack, or you'll have me to answer to."

"I got that covered," Jack responded. "Call us along the way!" he yelled as she drove off.

Dax turned to Mac and Brad. "Can we convince you guys to meet up with us in Key West in a few weeks?" he asked.

"Who knows," Brad said. "I would love some sandy beaches and hot sunsets."

"Me too," Mac added. "Maybe, so let's keep in touch."

They all walked to the plane together, said their good-byes, and Mac and Brad taxied out to the harbor. Dax and Jack stood in the sunshine and watched the floatplane disappear into the fluffy, white clouds.

They spent the next few days interviewing boat brokers and slowly packing up what little Jack would take with him to Key West. He and Dax had decided to call Portland home, so he'd sent most of his things on the truck with Dona. He'd figured that, since he'd called the *Lindsey C* home for so many years, he might actually like to have a real home, especially one with Dax in it. So the decision was an easy one.

When the cab pulled up at the dock to take them to the airport, Jack handed the boat keys to the broker, and he and Dax got into the cab and drove off into their new life together.

SCOTTY CADE left Corporate America and twenty-five years of marketing and public relations behind to buy an inn & restaurant on the island of Martha's Vineyard with his partner of fourteen years.

He started writing stories as soon as he could read, but only recently for publication. When not at the inn, you can find him on the bow of his boat writing male/male romance novels with his Shetland sheepdog Mavis at his side. Being from the South and a lover of commitment and fidelity, most of his characters find their way to long, healthy relationships, however long it takes them to get there. He believes that in the end, the boy should always get the boy.

Scotty and his partner are avid boaters and live aboard their boat, spending the summers on Martha's Vineyard and winters in Charleston, SC, and Savannah, GA.

Visit Scotty at http://www.scottycade.com and Facebook. You can contact him at Scotty@scottycade.com.

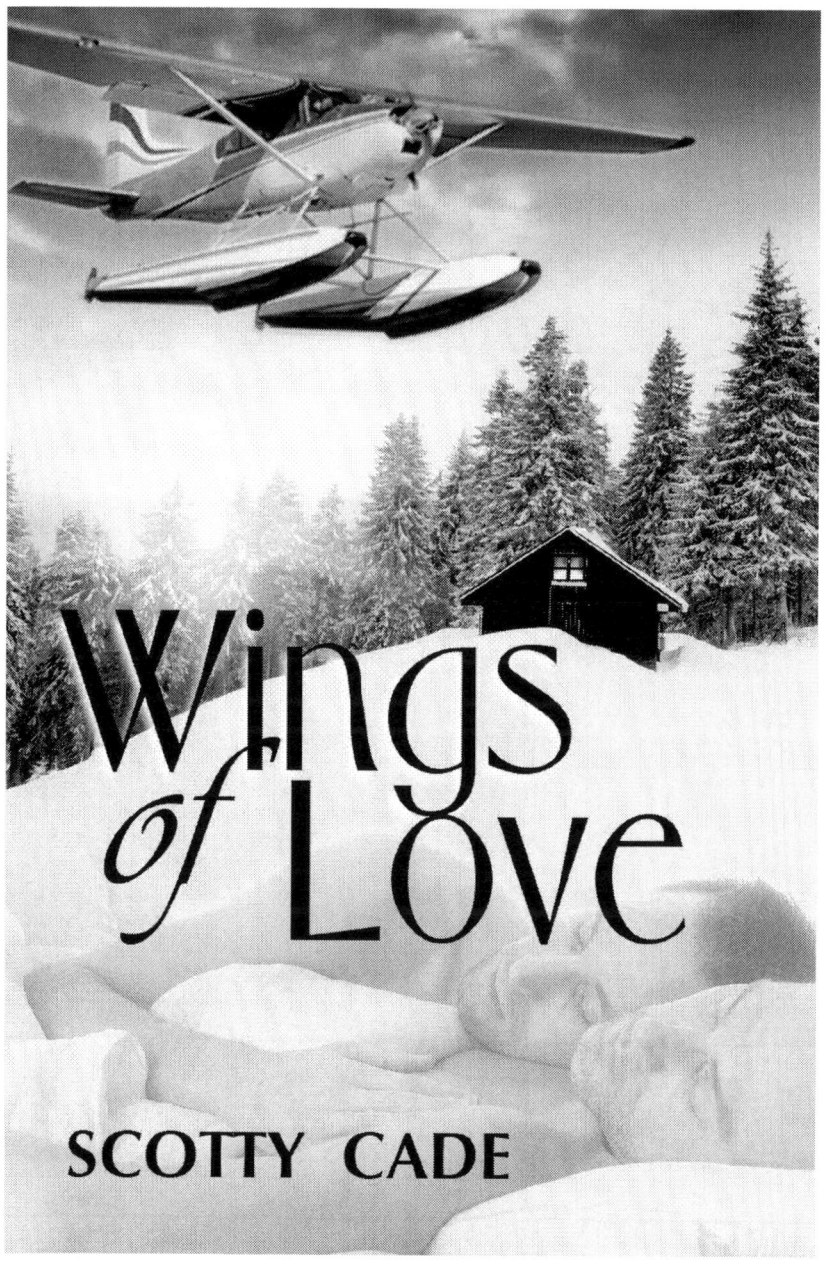

Also from SCOTTY CADE

Romance from DREAMSPINNER PRESS

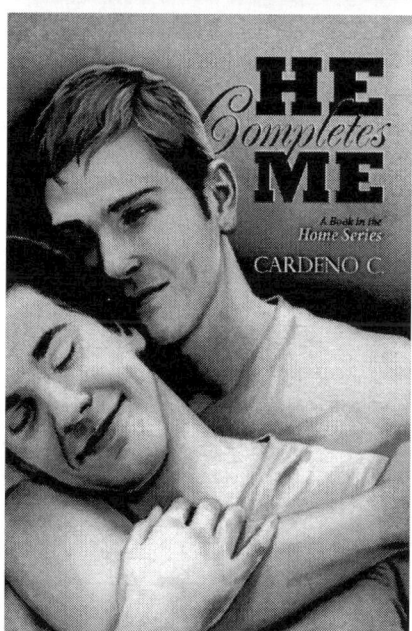

Made in the USA
Coppell, TX
29 October 2021

64874598R00118